FREE RIDE

SHADOW KEEPERS MC

M.N. FORGY

Free Ride brings to light a lot of what people go through with this condition, but this story is fiction and doesn't in any way demonstrate to the full extent of what someone with Dissociative Identity Disorder goes through.

DEDICATION

FIND SOMETHING YOU LOVE, AND LET IT KILL YOU.

Love is hard to find. Whether it's with someone, or something, it's a rare full body emotion that not many get to experience. It won't be ordinary, in fact it won't be like anything else you've ever known. So, if you find it, love it with everything you have. Even if it kills you in the end. Because you'll die happy... right?
Just don't judge its dents and scratches when you come across your something, because that's what makes it special... or fucking crazy.

In Memory of Sara Burch
If you were here, you would be reading this before anyone else and telling me how I'm your MC Queen. It feels odd publishing a book without you by my side. So in memory of you my friend, know I think of you while publishing this book.
Xoxo

PROLOGUE

HARLEY

Six Years Old

The bottoms of my dirty feet stick to the grimy discolored carpet as I make my way down the dark hallway to Mommy's room. The familiar smell of mold and Marlboro cigarettes, the scent I call home. Lifting my right arm, I run my fingers along the rough fake wood that makes up the walls of our single wide trailer. I hear moaning coming from the end of the hall, or maybe it's crying.

Pressing my hand on the flimsy door to Mommy's room, I push it open gently and peek through the small gap. The door is so worn out its hinges have begun to buckle and it won't shut all the way. My mouth parts and I breathe heavy as I spy. My mother's bare back faces me, her hair bouncing up and down as her body bobs up and down. My eyes fall to a man lying underneath her, but all I can make of his face is his sharp beak-like nose and hairy cheeks. The room smells funny, not matching the smell of the rest of the house either.

I blink slowly, taking in the scene. One I've seen before, but I still don't know what they're doing. Something naughty, I'm sure. I've seen bits of similar acts on TV.

It's not unusual to have strange men in Mommy's bedroom. She has lots of guys over that are *friends*. I'm not allowed in her room when they're over, but she's had lots of *friends* over today and I'm thirsty and hungry. I've already been through the fridge. Besides the milk jug that looks like it's about to explode from being old, there's nothing to eat.

Swallowing, my dry tongue feels like a fish out of water, reminding me why I went against Mommy's rules and came into her room when she had visitors in the first place.

Pushing the door the rest of the way open, I take a large breath to gain my courage and lift my chin.

"Mommy, can I have a glass of water, please?" I ask, swinging my hips, I make my purple dress flare at the bottom and I clutch the lapels of my leather jacket Daddy got me, as I display my outfit for mommy. I hope she likes it. I may not look right wearing such a grim jacket with a dress, but it's just my way. Much like my mother, I am different. Mother wears a bra and torn shorts everywhere, and tells everyone 'if they don't like it, don't look.' I like to match something pretty with black.

My mom is brave, which is why all the guys look at her the way they do. I want to be brave like her.

Mommy's head snaps in my direction, and she pulls the blankets to her bare chest. The bags under her eyes almost as dark as her wig, she glares at me. Feeling hot all of a sudden, I look to the dresser where she keeps her five wigs to avoid her angry stare. I like the pink and brown wig more than any of them. She should wear that one, it makes her skin glow.

"God, Harley, can't you do it yourself?" she growls, pushing herself up off the bed. She's naked, and very skinny compared to other moms I've seen. She reminds me of one of those skeletons you see people hang on their front door around Halloween. It's scary.

"I can't reach the glasses," I remind her. Last time I pushed the chair up to the counter she got very mad that I was going through the cabinets. I think she has something in a coffee can in the far right cabinet. It's the only thing in there, and I can't get the lid off. It's heavy and smells terrible. When you look through the plastic lid, all I see is white powder though. So why would she try and hide it?

Grabbing the pack of cigarettes off her nightstand, she plucks on with her thin lips and lights it. Smoke dances around her before she quickly blows smoke into the air.

"I'll be back," she mutters to the guy beside her. He's got his arm over his face, and blankets wrapped around his body. Standing completely naked, Mom stomps past me. Rolling my lips onto one another, I swirl my dress and follow her into the kitchen, the floor of our trailer creaking beneath our dirty feet as we head toward the kitchen.

"Did you see the outfit I changed into? I was bored, so I decided to change," I tell her, but she doesn't say anything. I stop in my tracks near Mom's small leather purse, the yellow and blue wrapper catching my attention. It's Double Bubble gum! Mom always has a piece in her purse the day after she comes home late from the bar. One time I got caught taking it, Mom told me a nice old guy at the bar always gives it to her. As nice as he is, he's creepy she says. It's the only candy I get around here, so I don't care how creepy the guy is. Flicking my gaze to make sure she's not looking, I reach into her purse and grab it. Quickly unwrapping it, I pop it in my mouth. Mouthwatering sugar coats my mouth. If the color pink had a taste, this would be it. Closing my eyes, I take a deep breath as my teeth chomp into the gum over and over. Kicking the wrapper under the couch, I follow Mom into the kitchen.

Mom sniffles, running her hand under her nose as she grabs a dirty glass from the sink. Filling it with water, you can see specks of dirt and food swirling around. My nose curls; it's not clean.

Mother looks at me with a cigarette hanging from her lips, her left eye squinted from the smoke.

"That kind of looks dirty, Mommy." Her eye opens all the way, and she scowls at me as if I'm the scum on our kitchen floor. I wring my fingers nervously. *Is she mad at me?*

"What's wrong?" I ask with a frown. She always looks at me like she's angry at me. I was really nice when I told her the glass was dirty. I don't want to get sick, again.

With pursed lips, she suddenly tosses the cold, dirty water on my face. I tense with shock as coldness soaks my dress and chills me to the bone. My heart sinks into my stomach reminding me of the day I ate too many cookies and drank a whole glass of milk at Daddy's.

She flicks her cigarette into the sink and it sizzles until the rising smoke stops.

My eyes sting, and my bottom lip trembles. I won't cry. I won't cry.

"Ask me for another glass of water!" she seethes through yellow teeth.

Warm tears roll down my face like a waterfall. My feelings hurt, and sadness locking around my chest to where breathing is a chore. "Do you want a glass of water, Harley?" The way she says my name compares to someone describing a cockroach. She hates me.

I blow the water off my lips and continue to cry where I stand. My pretty outfit is ruined.

"You look ridiculous in that jacket. Take it off!" she demands, pulling at the pretty leather recklessly. I pull away from her fearing she might tear it. If she rips it, I would be so sad. It's my favorite piece of clothing. Daddy got it for me for my birthday.

"Mommy, please let-let go," I breathe in as my chest begins to burn with anger. I knew I should have just gotten water from the tub and not bothered her.

"Little girls wear dresses, Harley!" She finally lets go and points at me, her thin eyebrows pinched together. "They like boys, and want fucking fairy tales and some shit!" Grabbing her wig, she slips it off her head and tosses it on the counter before running her fingers through her oily hair. "Who am I kidding, you'll never have what it takes to be a normal girl."

Normal little girls watch Disney movies, and want happily ever afters with handsome men, according to mom. But I would rather watch Beyond The Law, and Gone In Sixty Seconds. Those are real love stories.

My happily ever after lives in the hands of a man full of action, and is questionably the bad guy in the story.

"Get out of my sight!" she snaps.

Turning on my heel, I hurry out of the kitchen and quickly run into my room and scurry under my small bed. Shuffling myself further into the darkness that has become my escape since I can remember. I get comfortable in my secret fort and wipe a tear from my cheek. I pull my mermaid plushy close to me and watch a black bug crawl across the floor. The cobwebs and spiders don't bother me anymore; if anything, they hide with me. The beetle squeezes into a crack splitting up the wall and I reach my hand out running my finger along the splintered wood. I wish the bugs would take me with them sometimes. To hide in the dark and look out and watch when I wanted; to not be seen unless I want to.

Pulling the rainbow mermaid inside my leather jacket, the memory of when I unwrapped the jacket and stuffed toy replay in my head. It's one of the few good memories I have. I got them both for my birthday from my dad, who I don't often see because his job is dangerous. He's a biker.

Sitting at the wobbly table in our kitchen, I swing my feet back and forth waiting for Daddy to show up. Today is my birthday, and I'm so excited. I'm five.

"You think the place looks okay?" Mommy asks as she smooths her

hands down her thin spring dress. She looks pretty today. She doesn't usually wear dresses. It must be for Daddy.

"I think it looks cleaner than ever!" I throw my hands out in excitement. She growls words under her breath, and I shrink into my seat. She's always so angry, maybe she needs more naps.

The door swings open and the smell of something herbal and leather rush into the old trailer. It's Dad. I know that smell from anywhere. My eyes widen, my heart racing as I sit up in my chair.

Dad stepped further into the trailer carrying two packages wrapped with different colored balloons. Pushing out of my chair I ran to him, nearly knocking him over. He dropped the gifts to the ground and hugged me so tightly I felt safe for the first time in a long time.

"Happy birthday, princess," he whispers into my head, and I squeeze him tighter.

"Can I open them?" Pulling back, I look up at him before looking at the gifts on the floor in excitement.

"Go for it," he chuckles. I dropped to my knees, and I tore into the wrapping.

Pulling free a bright colored mermaid, I squealed and hugged her to my chest

"I love her!!" Quickly I dove into the next one, and the black shiny leather made me gasp. I held it up and lost all my words.

Dad hunched down, running his finger along the sleeve.

"You're the princess of my club, you need your own jacket."

Still in shock, I looked at my daddy.

"Can I be in your club?"

He laughed as if I told a joke, and stood up. I wasn't joking though. I wanted to be in Daddy's club, and I would be.

My mother didn't get me anything, but I was told to lie to Dad and tell him she did. I didn't care though, dad got me the best gifts ever. Something pretty, and something black.

I sniffle as I come back out of the happy memory, I wish dad was here right now. I wish Daddy would take me away from this place. He tells me it's too dangerous to live with him, but if he only knew how cranky Mommy is maybe he'd take me to his club where I know I belong.

I close my eyes, pretending I'm not Harley. That I'm someone else, someone Mommy likes, maybe even loves. Her perfect little girl, in a perfect world.

———

I HEAR GLASS BREAK, and my eyes snap open. I yawn and find myself in complete darkness. My body is pressed together like a pretzel in a small space. I'm not under my bed anymore. My heart beats fast, my ears ringing from the silence. Standing up on tingly legs, I feel around in the darkness.

"MOMMY!" I scream in panic, but I hear nothing in reply. I feel a knob on what I think is a door and push. Light blinds me, and I realize I'm in my closet.

Blinking confused, I step out and stare at the bed, then the closet. I wonder how I got from under my bed into the closet. This isn't the first time I've blacked out before. I've been waking up in odd places a lot lately.

"Where is she?" The familiar voice of Daddy sounds through the small trailer. My eyes light up, a smile spreading across my small face. Dad!

"Why are you here?" Mom's hatred heavy in her voice

"Jesus, look at this fucking place, do you ever clean, Kelsey?"

"Maybe I would have if I knew you were coming over!" Mommy hollers back. The walls are so thin it sounds as if she's right in the room with me.

"The fucking neighbor called me, I gave her my number in case Harley needed me. She said Harley asked her for food late last night?" I stiffen, Mrs. Boomer promised she wouldn't tell anyone. I was sitting on the front steps, and a pizza man delivered her food. The smell was so good, I couldn't help but ask for a slice.

"She's fine, Grudge! Just give me the money so we can get some groceries or something, and leave!" Mommy snaps. She won't spend it on groceries though. I don't know where the money goes, but it's not on food.

"Daddy!" I cry happily, running down the dark narrow hallway. He's so tall his head tickles the ceiling, his lips slowly pulling into a smirk as he watches me run to him.

He turns, his green eyes falling upon me. They're so warm, so loving. Like green vines wrapping me so tightly, I know nothing could cut through them.

"Baby girl!" he states in a low rugged voice. He hunches down and scoops me up in his big arms in a cheerful manner. His hand firmly tucks behind my head pulling me in closer. The familiar smell of leather smothers me, and I nuzzle my nose inside his neck. When I'm scared or hiding under my bed, I often think of this smell. I tell myself one day I will be just like Daddy and ride a motorcycle.

He sniffs me, and I feel his body tense beneath me as he gently pulls away.

"Hey, why don't you go get your things. Hmm?"

I give Mommy a quick look before agreeing. He slides me to my feet, and I hesitantly head to my room.

He seemed so happy to see me, now he looks angry.

"Don't you look at me like that! You can't take her!" Mommy screams, flying at my dad in a fit of anger. I stop where I stand, frozen to the floor as I watch my parents fight.

"What have you been doing with the money I've been giving you, Kelsey, because you ain't feeding her! When was the last time she even bathed?" Daddy roars.

"She's had lots of friends over, Daddy," I try to defend Mom. His eyes widen and he scowls at Mommy.

"You're tricking again?"

Mom sucks in a breath, looking at me horrified.

"Do you know how dangerous that is for Harley? What if one

of them—" As if he can sense me standing here watching, his head whips in my direction.

"Harley, don't make me repeat myself. Get your shit and get it now!" he barks in an angry tone causing goosebumps to break out against my skin from the chill in his voice.

Blinking rapidly, I turn and run to my room, grabbing my mermaid and leather jacket from under the bed. I look around, silently hoping I'll never return. Shutting the door behind me I say goodbye to the bugs, and take in a deep breath before heading back to the living room.

"All ready." I smile. Mom and Dad look at me with red faces, I can tell they're still fighting.

Dad slides his hand through his dark hair and plasters a fake smile on his face.

"Go with Roadie." His hand swings toward the door, where Roadie stands. I didn't even notice he was in here with all the excitement. Roadie is tall and skinny. Blond and black hair flopping in his face. "I'll be at the clubhouse in a bit, baby. I have some shit to take care of first," Daddy informs, glaring at Mommy. She must be in trouble.

I look to Roadie with a nervous smile. I've only seen him once before when Daddy took me for ice cream. He didn't talk much but would always smile at me when he caught me looking at him. He seemed friendly.

Roadie clasps my hand gently, whispering for me to follow him outside.

I struggle, wanting to wait for Daddy. I want to ride on his motorcycle, not ride in a car with Roadie!

"Go, Harley," Dad insists. My brows furrow, my lips pinching together in anger.

Jerking my hand from Roadie's, I frown and lead the way outside. Roadie sighs loudly and follows me outside onto the old porch. The same one that shoved a splinter the size of a pencil in the bottom of my foot last summer. I was crying and bleeding so badly the landlord across the street pulled it out with some tool from his garage and taped my foot up with duct tape. I showed the girl down the street the scar and she ran to her house crying. I'm the toughest kid in this trailer park.

In a shiny black car parked right out front of our ugly green trailer, I see a little boy with dark hair looking out the backseat window, his breathing fogging the glass. I stop on the bottom wooden step and look back at him. I haven't been around kids my age much, especially boys. I'm homeschooled, which consists of me watching discovery channel every day, and the flashcards Mom bought at the Dollar Tree. I know every card, but I still quiz myself every day.

"KEEP MOVING, HARLEY." Roadie presses on my back. Swallowing the sudden lump forming in my throat, I make myself move off the bottom step.

Getting closer to the car, the boy in the back seat smiles a crooked grin, and my cheeks warm. I bet if I looked in a mirror they'd be pink.

He waves, and I hesitantly wave back. My heart grows a mind of its own, beating faster than I've ever felt before as I wipe my sweaty palms on my dress.

"Come on, you can sit next to my boy, Benjamin." Roadie opens the door for me, and the boy now known as Benjamin smiles at me like nobody has ever smiled at me before. He has dark hair falling in his face, and bright blue eyes staring at me with excitement. Wow, his eyes look just like the color crayon I use to fill in the ocean in my old coloring book.

He's wearing a long-sleeved Captain America T-shirt and camouflaged shorts. His knees are bruised and scuffed up, and I can't help but notice his black boots are untied with the laces dangling down the sides. I really like those leather boots, they'd go well with my jacket. Climbing into the car, I slide along the leather seat and sit as far away from him as I can.

"You can call me Benji!" Benjamin says, scooting closer to me. I swallow harder, my teeth pinched together at his closeness. My spine is straight, my shoulders stiff. My eyes flick back and forth from the seat in front of me to him. *Why is he so friendly? He hardly knows me. Are all kids this nice?*

"I'm ten, how old are you?" he asks, not catching on to my unease.

"I'm- I'm six," I reply quietly. My hands clench onto one another in my lap, my chest feeling like someone released a jar of butterflies.

"I'm older, so you have to listen to me." He crosses his arms, his chin lifted high. I scowl, the butterflies going up in flames.

"No, I don't," I snap, my face twisted in anger.

"Yes, you do. I have to protect you. That's how it works, the boy protects the girl, duh." He rolls his eyes. Huffing, I cross my arms.

"That is dumb, who says the girl even needs a boy to protect her? Maybe the boy is the one who needs the girl to save and protect him."

His blue eyes turn a shade darker, and he looks confused.

"Wait! Come back, Harley!" Mommy cries. I look over Benji's shoulder, just as Dad steps out onto our broken porch and stands behind Mommy, his face hard and unfriendly. Dad grips Mommy by the arm, pushes her inside the trailer like a ragdoll.

"Say goodbye to Mommy, Harley." Dad gives me a hard look.

"Bye, Mommy..." My words are lost on my tongue. Fear for her knotting in my stomach.

"What is Daddy doing with Mom?" I ask Roadie who is now behind the wheel.

"Oh, things are just getting heated is all," he informs with a bored tone.

Lifting up on my knees I look out the back window at the

trailer. Will I ever see Mommy again? I know my mom is not the best mom in the world, but she's still my mom. The idea that I'll miss her surprises me, and my eyes begin to well with tears.

A cold hand rests on top of mine, and my head whips down to Benji looking up at me with sad eyes.

"It's okay, you got me."

Swallowing the tears back, I slide back into my seat as Roadie pulls the black car away from the trailer.

1

TWENTY YEARS LATER

Harley

A large callused hand grasps the nape of my neck, the familiar smell of leather, weed, and whiskey wafting around me. That smell should be put in a candle, it'd sell a shit load the way it eases the anxiety in one's chest.

A hard, warm body presses up against my back, and my eyes nearly roll into the back of my head.

"Benji." The name falls from my tongue like a moan midst ecstasy. He feels so good against my body, my mind nearly loses its reality.

His lips brush against my ear. His hands slowly, lazily, slip down the back of my jeans, and his fingers brush against my sex. Tingles of pleasure surround my wetness, the notion to forget what is right and wrong nearly a breath in the wind with his hands on me.

"I want to bite this ass, trail my tongue down your supple cheeks until I dive my tongue deep inside this hot cunt of yours," he mutters.

I grit my teeth with temptation. I want to wrap my legs

around his neck while he licks every drop of my wetness. My body clenching around his tongue as I release what I've been denying myself into his mouth. I want to let him mouth fuck me into another world where it's just him and I... but that would be selfish of me. A fucking mess.

I could lose him.

I grab him by the wrist and pull his hand out from my bottoms, his finger leaving a trail of wetness behind it.

"You can't say my name like that, and deny me that tight ass, Harley," he growls into the back of my ear.

"We can't do this, you know that." I clear my throat and shake my head.

There's no denying that Benji is a catch. Tall, dangerous, and smoldering eyes that make you want to throw the idea of wearing panties into a fire.

But, I'm not capable of having a traditional relationship. I'm not saying that to be that teasing bitch everyone knows. I'm just the kind of girl that doesn't get to experience the glamorous kind of love. No, my heart comes with a little bloodshed and a shot of insanity on the side. That's the biker's way of life, after all, and that alone makes me bad at this thing called love. I can't promise I won't break his heart. If I did lose him as my best friend, it'd be the first thing I'd never forgive myself for. Even if I did tease him, you couldn't blame me. Benjamin Daxton is the sexiest man in this club.

I'm not mentally stable to love Benji.

My eyes water as I think about the first time I realized I'd never be good enough for Benji.

Waking up in an uncomfortable position, I sit up. My vision blurred, my head pounds and my mouth is dry. I notice I am in the backseat of some truck I've never seen before. The smell of stale beer and Old Spice deodorant making me want to vomit. The material of the black dress I didn't know I even owned, makes my skin itch and sweat, and I pull at it impatiently as I try to figure out how I got in that truck.

The sound of someone heaving in the front seat has me sitting forward. Looking over the vinyl blue bench seat, I find a young man with tattoos all over his back throwing up in the floorboard. I've never seen him before. How did I get here? Did we do anything sexual? God, I hope not.

"Why am I here?" I ask with a shaky voice. Scared of what he's going to say. My heart flutters with the words about to fall from his dry lips.

He coughs, wiping his face with his forearm. His face is pale and his eyes are hooded like he's smoked too much.

"I was going to show you a good time, but I got sick, babe." He shakes his head with embarrassment.

Rage sobers me instantly. My eyes filling with tears as I jerk the door open and slam it shut.

There's no way I would let this happen. He's not even cute!

"Hey, let me get your number!" the boy's who name I don't even know, suggests. He doesn't know who I am or he wouldn't be asking me so bluntly. He has no idea I'm the president's daughter. It's refreshing but dangerous.

"HARLEY!" I hear Benji yell from the clubhouse. Looking at the boy in the truck, I furrow my brows. My heart beating a mile a minute.

"You better leave. Now!" If Benji finds him, he'll kill him. He will drag him out of his truck, and pound his fist in this boy's face over and over again. Then my dad will take the back tire to his Harley across his face.

I see the passion in Benji's eyes, I know he wants to be with me. To see me with someone else... it would kill him.

Benji groans as if I just took his dick from him and slammed it in a drawer, grabbing me from the trip down memory lane. A memory I remember often, because it's permanent tattoo of why I can't be with him.

I have Dissociative Identity Disorder, also known as split personality. It ruins my life in some ways, such as having a real relationship with anyone. So, when Benji looks at me like I'm the only girl in his world... there's really more. Harley, which is my front personality and then my alter that calls herself Farrah. Farrah has been a part of my life ever since I can remember. She's the other half of me. When she comes forward, she's always altering my appearance to something sweet and innocent, though she's anything but. She's a slut in a flower dress, and I can't stand it when she puts me in clothing that reveals so much of my skin. I don't know anything she does when she comes to the front, I just black out. It's like swimming through a dark abyss as I wait to come to the front in a different place, in different clothes, confused as fuck.

Benji pulls away from me, and I turn to face him. My face flushed and I place my hands on the dresser behind me in attempt to keep them from grabbing at Benji's hard body.

"What are you guys talking about today? Are you going on a run? Do you need some help?" I fire a series of questions at him. The club is about to have a meeting and I want to go so bad, I've wanted to go since I was a little girl. I'm the Shadow Keepers' MC princess, and my crown is my helmet. I want to be a part of the club so bad. When I was younger, Benji and I would hide under the wooden table from time to time, but we eventually got bigger, and got caught. My dad made it a habit of checking under the table after that, and I haven't been back in there since. Benji has been in there since though because my dad patched him in.

He steps in where needed, the club muscle if you will. The size of Benji's shoulders and arms, it's a no-brainer to make him the Shadow Keepers' enforcer.

Benji's shoulders are wide and built with muscle, his arms tattooed and thick. He's the king of pain and it's scary what his charming smile can hide. You'd never know he was a murderer if he wore a suit and tie. That's how handsome and dangerous he really is.

"You can't come and you know that." Benji slides my blonde hair behind my ear. His touch soft but firm.

His ocean eyes bore into mine, searing me where I stand as if I'm the only girl in the world. The feeling is warm and fuzzy, and a façade. I'm not the only girl in his world. If I was, maybe things would be different between us.

My eyes fall along his sharp face. The dark stubble on his chin causes my fingers to twitch with the urge to run both of my palms over it just to feel the scratch of it on my fingers. His shaggy black hair falls in his eyes when he looks at me. Trundles that are lighter in color from riding in the sun too much curl around the tops of his ears.

He notices my lingering stare and flicks his nose with his thumb, his tongue sliding along his bottom lip as he looks at me with hooded eyes. His smoldering blue orbs too intense to look at, my eyes fall to the scar on the bridge of his nose. It's lighter than the rest of his tanned skin demonstrating even though he's beautiful, he's an unpredictable man. I remember the day he got that scar. A club passing through stopped at the Shadow Keepers go to spot for whiskey. The Rolling Barrels Pub. The other club disrespected our club's colors, and Benji got heated and got in his face. The man from the opposing club punched Benji right in the face and broke his sunglasses; slicing his nose wide open. Benji broke the man's right arm after that, and there's no pain for a biker like not riding their motorcycle.

It was one of the few times I got to leave the club, and I witnessed the whole club fight that night. I'll never forget how much Benji looked like a monster and less like a man.

Benji and I grew up together, MC brats. Both schooled and confined within the walls of the Shadow Keepers MC. My home is just above the clubhouse my father is the president of. Benji's dad, Roadie, is the VP and they both live downstairs in two of the club's rooms. Benji is my best friend, we do everything together. Just not runs or anything club related.

The Shadow Keepers' clubhouse was founded in Arizona by my father. He came back from the war a lost man and not only homeless but jobless. He stumbled upon a condemned home by a beach and slowly rebuilt it. Other lost souls joined him, and they began to get into pot running and before they knew it, they became the Shadow Keepers.

They're a motherfucking legend around here. A club named Tail Chasers used to run this side of Arizona. They sold weak pot and some cheap guns. Eventually, Dad moved in on their territory and wiped them out with better weed, and eventually better stock in guns. Many have tried to take out the Shadow Keepers, and many have gone missing trying. Keep your competition six feet under, and you'll always remain on top.

"Meet me on the roof after the meeting?" he asks with a low rugged tone. We always head to the roof, smoke a blunt and talk bullshit after club meetings. But tonight, my palm aches to hold a .45. My heart beats to the sound of the clicking mechanism of an automatic weapon. I'm programmed to wreak havoc and leave a path of blood in my wake. Nobody can stop that, not even the code of the club.

I'm becoming restless being sheltered in this fucking club.

"This is bullshit," I grumble shaking my head. My eyes fall to my bed with the club colors printed on the bedding.

"The day a woman sits at the table, is the day the legacy of biker clubs around the world die. You know that," Benji quotes my father, but his tone of voice lacks the belief in that sentence. I flick a brow up at him, his words insulting and out of line.

The very thought that I will never be in that room weighing heavy on my shoulders, I lash out the only way I know how.

Grabbing the red lamp on my night table, I throw it at him. He ducks, the lamp barely missing him, and he gives me a sideways glance as if I'm crazy. It's ironic, as we both know I'm past crazy. There's no cure for what I have. I'm the bitch with the leather jacket, matching boots, and joint hanging out of her mouth as I drive the fucking crazy train through the image portrayed for what a lady is to act like.

"It's not healthy for you to be around violence," he raises a brow, repeating what my therapist has told me.

"I get it. I'm a fucking nutcase," I sneer, pointing to my head. There's a darkness inside of me that weaves and vines through my limbs, and when my heart pounds to the rhythm of someone hurting, or I get a waft of spilled blood. That darkness blooms within me past unstoppable. Members of the club have told me I scare my own father, and that hurts. I refuse to believe I frighten him, I should make him proud. The DNA of what he stands for runs deep inside of my body, nothing will stop me until I am at that table.

Benji growls. "You know I hate it when you fucking call yourself that. You're just... different, Harley, and your dad doesn't want you around club shit. It brings the worst out of you," he clarifies.

What does he want me to say? That 'I'll change?' Be a good girl who likes to decorate and bake cookies? That I'll look the other way of innocent blood shed as I step over the empty bullet casings serving beer to club members?

I won't be that woman. Ever.

"I won't give up my self-respect just to make people who think they love me, feel normal," I growl in reply. His eyes widen with insult.

"And you think I'm one of those people that want you to change?"

My brows furrow inward with uncertainty. I didn't think he used to be one of those people, but the way he quotes my dad so often anymore... I'm not so sure. I'm hoping he's just telling himself I am better left up here so that one day he will believe it himself.

"You better get going, Dad will bust your face if he finds you in here again." I look over my shoulder with a grave expression. Benji knows he's not allowed in my room, if Dad heard him in here it'd be both of our asses.

Shaking his head, he walks out of the room, slamming my

door behind him. My shoulders tense from the loud echo of the door.

Sometimes I cannot believe he agrees with the rest of the club, or should I say my fucking father. That's something that makes me question him. He's always pushing for more between us, yet when push comes to shove, he takes my father's words as his bond.

"No woman will ever be patched in." I hear my father's voice echo through my brain. I have more balls then the crew my father has behind him.

My loyalty runs blood deep, and the fact I have a pussy is blinding anyone from seeing that. This club is who I am, it's who I've always been.

I just need to prove myself I have what it takes to stand with the rest of them. Then they will all see a woman is just as worthy to sit at the club table as a man. Raising my hand, my fingers fumble with my bottom lip in thought.

I stall, my eyes widening with a brilliant idea.

That's just it, I need to *prove* I'm strong. A chance to show them that I can be trusted to do what is needed to be my dad's right hand. It's 2018, times of change. Why can't a woman sit at the table, ride a motorcycle, and be a patched-in member? Especially if she proves she has what it takes just as much as any other man at the table?

I jerk the door open, and quickly head down the stairs, determined to make my dad give me a job. The doors to the chapel are closed, meaning church is already in session. Church as in, this where they hold their meetings and daily business. I'd do anything to be at the table, to hear where they're going, who they're hurting, and what is to come at the hands of the Shadow Keepers. I want to see who falls to their knees at the mercy of my family, to see the fear seep from someone who crossed us. I can't sit idle a moment longer, I need excitement. I need ... to find my place in this world.

We're all sinners here, yet I'm the only one everyone walks around like a sacred angel that might break at any moment. I'm no fucking angel.

I carefully press my ear to the metal door to listen in. These doors were crafted from old boat docks nearby, and are thick. Making it hard to hear anything. Still. This might be the closest I've been to that table in a long time. My heart pounds so loudly I gently place my hand on the swell of my chest trying to calm myself so I can hear what's being said.

"Governor Timothy hasn't paid us back. He still owes us ten grand for making that leader protesting the rebuild on the Animosity Community, disappear," my dad informs the table. My mouth parts hearing we killed a protestor to help a governor. There has been a lot of speculation on the television about his backroad ways, and if he's in with our club then he's definitely messed up.

"That build wiped out a lot of wildlife." Viper's tone grim, and I frown thinking about all the animals losing homes. Viper is one of the younger men at the table and has a fascination with snakes. I hear he has a poisonous viper in his room, but that's not why they call him Viper. One time last year he walked through the club with a bottle of half-filled Jack Daniels bottle in one hand and was completely naked. I caught a glimpse of a snake tattoo winding up the side of his hard body. A viper to be exact. My spoon fell into my bowl of Fruit Loops as I've never seen a naked man look so beautiful before, the clinking sound caught his attention and he winked at me as he continued his way through the clubhouse as if his erect cock wasn't swinging freely. It was so long, it could be a snake. So it begs the question. Do they call him Viper because of his lengthy cock, or is it because of the tattoo?

He's the Sergeant at Arms. You need a weapon, he has it. I hear his room has guns of all sorts on the walls. I've tried to pick the lock to see for myself, but it's impenetrable.

"Aw, look. Viper grew a vagina," Roadie teases Viper for caring about the demolition of nature. Roadie is our road captain and just happens to be Benji's dad. I've known him a long time. He's getting older in age though, I don't think he will be able to lead many more rides due to his sore hands and back. I head the last ride they went on they had to keep stopping to give Roadie's hands a break.

"Are you wanting to fuck me now, Roadie? I knew you were fucking gay," Viper strikes back.

"Only if there's a tight pussy in between those ass cheeks," Roadie replies seriously.

"Enough," Dad orders the banter to stop. "He has threatened to burn down our club, and turn us over to the police if we retaliate in any way," my father informs his men. This news makes my nostrils flare. This is my home, my life. Surely my father won't just sit back and let this man breathe after such grave threats.

I bite my bottom lip as I listen in, my ear nearly suction-cupped to the door.

"We should send a warning," Bridge states. Bridge is one of those men that look like they just got out of prison. Hairy, tattooed, and built. He's quiet, and mysterious too. Only thing that breaks that outlaw look is the fact he hates driving his bike over bridges. Benji told me Bridge has driven an hour out of the way from the rest of the men just to avoid a fucking bridge. Nobody knows why he hates bridges, and if you ask, all you get is a serious, intense stare. Like he might snap your neck.

So, nobody asks anymore.

"Whatever we do, it has to be a smart move. Bold and quick so he can't follow through with his threats," Dad clarifies.

"You can't trust politicians," Viper sneers, and I roll my eyes. Viper doesn't know shit about politics, so his statement is vague as shit.

"Babe, what are you doing?" I snap upright, my spine stiff. I've been caught listening in to club business, which is a big lawbreaker of the Shadow Keepers. We don't have a lot of rules, but the ones we do have are firm and the law we live by. It's not like the laws normal citizens follow, those are trivial compared to ours if you disobey them. There is no hope for you here; you're fucked. I remember one time Benji and I sat on the stairs as we watched Roadie and my father take a blow torch to one of the member's backs burning off his club colors for underselling some of our top pot and keeping the profit. I'll never forget the smell. Benji tried to cover my eyes, but I wanted to watch. Something drew me to the violence and excited me.

The sound of Tickles clearing her throat makes me tense, and my head snaps in her direction. She's a club bitch and thinks she belongs here more than I because she sleeps with everyone. The men call her a club cunt, but I hate that fucking term just about as much as I hate her. She's got cherry red hair with blue streaks, and fake eyelashes so big they touch her thin eyebrows.

She's not fat, but not skinny. She has curves, and big breasts to match. I've seen her naked more than I'd like as she has no shame walking around without any clothes on.

I know I'm no good for Benji, but when Tickles gets around him and bats those lashes, it's like all the butterflies in my stomach die off one by one. I want to kill her.

Seeing Tickles stare at me as she waits for my response on why I am listening in to a chapter meeting has my hands rolling into fists. I want to hurt her, but even if she is just a club slut... she's one of ours and I can't touch her without repercussions.

"I was just seeing if they had started their meeting, I needed to ask my father something and didn't want to interrupt," I lie with a fake smile. She rolls her eyes and tucks herself behind the bar for a morning drink. Vodka with a splash of orange juice.

Daddies little psycho path," she mocks with an ugly face.

My nails dig into my palms as I glare in her direction. I hate being called that, and she always does it. I know it was her that scratched it into my bedroom door.

"You think those men are capable of savage acts?" I ask. "I will murder your whole family if you talk to Benji again." I threaten with a blank stare. She blinks slowly, her brain trying to process if I'm fucking with her or not.

Keeping my chin up, I make quick of my footwork, and I head back upstairs to our house. I grab my leather bag from the corner and start stuffing it full of clothes as quickly as I can. If my dad isn't going to protect this club with guns blazing, and won't trust me behind the table with him, then I will fucking do a job by myself. Without his consent.

I have to find my place in this world, and if breaking club law and going behind his and Benji's back is the only way... then so be it. They won't kill me for disobeying, I'm the club princess after all.

Pulling open my top drawer full of panties, I dump them on the floor, grabbing the pistol just before it clanks to the carpeted ground. Pulling the chamber open, I make sure it's loaded and shut it again. Dad doesn't know I have it, nobody does. I snatched it from Roadies' holster one night when he was so drunk he passed in the middle of taking a piss by the back door. He thinks a hang-around stole it. Which is something that is very likely to happen. A hang-around comes around when parties are going on, someone who wants in the club but hasn't shown their full worth yet. To have a gun from a Shadow Keeper, that is show and tell at its fucking finest.

Stepping out of my room I tiptoe down the stairs, look at the church door one last time, before running out the back of the club.

Bud stands just outside, making me skid to a stop.

"Bud," I say in surprise. Hat lowered, Bud looks up, eyes meeting mine before falling to my leather bag. Bud looks down before going inside and slamming the door. Bud knows I'm running and is letting me go.

I strengthen my hold on my bag. "We can do this," I

encourage myself. Pumping myself up for the journey ahead. I'm not going to lie, I'm scared as shit. I've never been outside these walls by myself.

The bus station is only a mile from here, I can make it on foot. Tossing my bag over my shoulder, I run. The night air is crisp and fills my lungs as I sprint away from the only thing I've ever known.

I'll prove them all wrong. I'll prove that I belong here. There is no other choice.

Running across the beach and the main highway I head to the bus station, looking over my shoulder the whole time. I'm so scared I'll get caught it's taking everything I have to hold down my dinner.

It's raining, thunder cracking in the sky as my clothes stick to my skin making it harder for me to run. Huffing out of breath, and freezing despite the heat, I finally make it. Trying to catch my breath I sit under the small awning and look the governor up on my phone, getting all the details I need to make him my target. A family picture of him, his wife, and who looks like maybe his daughter and her husband grab my attention.

The young man's hand is interlocked in the daughter's, as she smiles and waves as if she's fucking running for Miss America. The husband looks scared, miserable even.

I run my finger over my screen. Their clothes are so nice, their faces smooth and unknown of hardship.

They're privileged and that alone sparks a burning jealousy in my chest. The hardships of my life are badges of honor I wear proudly. It's proof I'm stronger than those who stick their nose up as they walk by.

The husband's shirt catches my attention as my finger slides over him. He's wearing a typical Arizona college shirt. You see young kids wearing them all the time, but this man looks to be in his thirties and doesn't look to be a college student in the least bit. I click a new browser open and Google the college and the professors. Finding his profile picture at the very top. I open it.

Professor Michael Prescott teaches American literature. Volunteering in the horticulture department as a passion on the weekends. He's married to June Prescott, the governor's daughter—

I stop there, tapping my foot in thought. Dad said we needed to be smart, but bold in our strike against the governor. Maybe instead of going at the governor directly, I should take what matters most to him. His family.

A family walks past me, and I fake a smile. A mother and father pass carrying a little girl. She has bouncy blonde pigtails and an old teddy bear hanging from one of her hands. The little girl looks over her dad's shoulder at me when they pass. Her eyes locked on mine.

"Hi!" The little girl waves at me, her bravery to talk to me taking me aback. The father looks over his shoulder and frowns when he sees me. "Don't talk to her, Lizzy," the father scolds, but that doesn't stop the girl from smiling at me. The mother and father quickly pick up their pace, as the father hugs his daughter tighter in pursuit of escaping the lone biker chick.

I cross my boot-clad feet, the shoelaces sticking to the wet concrete and look the other way. I'm used to it, but the way the father tried to protect his daughter makes me think twice about going after the governor's daughter. She'll be too protected by guards or something I'm sure. But what about the son in law? He's a man of no stature, and possibly too proud to lug around men to protect him.

I know shit about literature though unless you include the Harley manual in the garage that our mechanic Hairy had me read as a book report.

Turning my phone off, I go up to the window, with trembling hands I hand over a fifty. I'm scared, excited, and out of my mind being out here by myself, and doing what I'm about to do.

"I need a bus to the local college," I inform the old lady

behind a scratched -up plexiglass window, a cigarette hanging out of her mouth. She doesn't even look up from her Hollywood gossip magazine as she punches something into a machine before sliding me a ticket from under the window and taking my money. Grabbing the ticket, I turn where I stand, and look up at the big blue and white bus pulling up next to the station. I feel high with adrenaline, my teeth chattering with fear.

I should turn around. No, I'm going.

I can do this. I *am* doing this.

2

HARLEY

A couple hours later my clothes are still damp from the rainwater. Stepping off the main bus, I clutch my bag and look the campus over. I swallow hard, I've never been to school. Dad had Peachy and Big Hairy homeschool me, two older members of the club. When Big Hairy got to talking about politics, it got interesting to say the least. He's southern to the bone, and if you don't believe what he says, you better act like you do. However, my dad used what he had to educate me. Putting me in school was a risk he didn't want to play with. Having a split personality disorder, and though I have had it under control with medication for years... my father still thinks I'm a risk in public. Hence why I'm here to prove myself. I may not be able to walk down the sidewalk with society, grab a latte at the local Starbucks, or sit amongst a crowd of strangers in a theater, but that just means I'm meant to be on the back of a bike with a gun in my hand, slamming bullets into our enemies. Wearing the club colors proudly on my leather jacket is where my place is.

Chewing on my Double Bubble, I sink my teeth into the gum that presses through my lips.

The image of me riding my own motorcycle, and running from the police with the rest of the crew makes my brows curve with inspiration. A smile slips across my face as I become giddy. I've come thus far so I'm already in deep shit with my dad. I better pull this off to save my ass. Pulling the hood of my jacket over my head, I keep my head down and head inside the main office of the college.

Other people my age pass me, some staring at me, and one even runs into me, our shoulders bumping. Unease causes my spine to stiffen, and that sudden giddy feeling I had flees into tense defense.

"Watch it," flies out of my mouth before I can think twice, reminding me how far out of my element I truly am. I look at the ground, breathing deeply, trying to get a handle on my anger before I chase after the asshole who just bumped into me. If I was with the club, people wouldn't come within feet of us, the club colors on the brothers' cuts warning them off. Citizens not knowing who I am, or who I'm affiliated with makes me feel vulnerable. I have no protection, no one to keep me safe but myself.

My stomach knots and my breathing is forced as I try and stay focused on the task at hand. Getting enrolled under the radar and as smoothly as possible. If Dad or Benji know I'm here... they'll come for me. I have to keep my temper under control, keep my episodes of Farrah at bay. My alter personality.

I glance up from staring at the ground and see girls wearing barely nothing, even in the rain. Bright colors of clothing, and fancy shoes I couldn't afford in my lifetime all flash by me. I'm out of place here, and I can't help but feel like everyone is staring at me.

Once inside, my wet boots slop along the clean marble floor leaving behind muddy boot prints. Pulling my hood down off my head, I look at the mess I've created, a young girl with her tits hanging out of her sorority top looks at me in disgust as she sashays past.

"Shit," I mumble under my breath, taking a step back, I wipe my feet on the welcome mat. We don't have one of these at the club. Everyone just kicks the wall outside if we get too much crud on our boots, and if that doesn't help then a prospect mops the floors.

Sighing heavily, I lift my head from my feet, finding a young man with half his head shaved and a blue lip ring in this bottom lip, sitting behind the front desk. His eyes are bloodshot, and pupils dilated. He's a stoner, I can tell.

Stepping off the mat, my feet echo in the empty space.

The whole building is quiet, and it unnerves me. The clubhouse is rarely quiet. Men hollering, girls laughing, and the all-night parties of the club ensures a constant ruckus.

"Can I help you, angel?" the guy behind the desk asks with a devilish smirk. He looks me up and down as if I'm his next flavor and I laugh silently. If he thinks he can fuck me, he better think again. This devil wears heels so sharp they'll impale what's left of his brain cells.

"Wrong side of heaven." I tilt my head to the side, as I step up to him. Declaring I'm more of the dark angel rather.

As if he's shocked his charm didn't work, he stumbles on what he should say next. "I'd like to enroll." I don't give him a chance to recover.

His eyes narrow before resting his elbows on the counter. His head in his hands, his cheeks push his lips into an awkward shape.

"You know all the dorms are full, it's three weeks into the semester," he whispers the last part.

My gaze flicks to the side not sure what that means. This is all so new to me, maybe I should have Googled what to do before coming here. I wish Benji was here to help me with the one thing

I'm not good with. People. I'm not good at reading body language, the sarcasm in their voice is lost on me, and I get offended easily.

"You have your transcripts with you?" He lifts his chin, his stoned eyes looking at my wet breasts.

I open my mouth to speak but quickly close it. Do I have transcripts being homeschooled?

"I –"

"We can get you set up, but you need to get those faxed over before the end of the quarter for any credits to count." Shit, I'll have to see if I can find some fake ones or something. I bet I can pay someone off. One thing I've learned living the life of the club is everyone has a price.

"Residential-wise, I know of a dorm room right off the campus that just opened up, the tenant got arrested," he replies, bored, clicking the mouse and sliding it along the countertop.

"O-okay," I smile in acceptance.

"What will you give me?" he looks at me wolfishly. My mouth parts, my lip curling.

"I'm not sleeping with you!" I shout. If Benji was here, this man would have no teeth. I should knock his fucking teeth out myself. I can't though, I have to keep my cool. I blow out a calming breath. "How about a finder's fee or something?" I suggest nicely. I pull my bag around and pull out a hundred and slap it on the counter. Dad and the girls would pay me after club parties for helping here and there.

"That'll work," he chuckles like an idiot. "I mean, the place isn't in the best shape I hear, but it's perfect if you're in a pinch." Narrowing his stoned eyes at me he looks me up and down. "And I can tell you're in a pinch."

"Yeah, I'll take it." I nod, coming off like a bobblehead. I just need to get away from this guy before I break his nose.

"So, what is it? You trying to get away from the parents? Bad relationship or something?"

I chew on my gum harder, ignoring his questions. He's really nosey.

He must get the drift I'm not much of a talker, he looks back at the computer screen. "Let's see what we have for classes," he mumbles as he squints at the computer screen.

"I want in Professor Prescott's class," I mindlessly blurt. My cheeks warm as the guy looks at me with furrowed brows. *Smart move, Harley.*

"Um, okay," he replies slowly, the way his eyes look at me I can tell he's suspicious. I grit my teeth, stupid move on my part to seem so eager.

"I just, I heard he's a really good teacher is all," I shrug, trying to play it off. I smile and bat my lashes like Tickles does at the club.

"You know he's married, right?" He raises a brow at me, thinking I'm interested in boning the teacher. I fight against the smirk on the edge of my mouth. Sleep with the teacher? Fuck no, I'd much rather kill the teacher.

"Yes... I do," I drawl out, returning the glare.

"His wife volunteers therapy sessions here in the clinic once a week," he informs, and my eyes bulge at this news. I've done my research on the bus ride here, I knew the daughter of the governor was a highly sought after therapist in the area, but I didn't know she did volunteer work. Here!

I can't believe her father would let her wander around without being protected. Maybe I should be going after her instead of the professor. Direct fucking target like I had planned.

I bite my bottom lip to hide the excitement. This is going a lot easier than I thought.

"I'd like to sign up for her sessions as well," I inform with pursed lips.

3

FARRAH

ONE DAY LATER

B
lack fades from my vision, and I notice I'm not at the club. I'm in a small room I've never seen before. Slowly I walk to the window and look out it. Young adults with backpacks and books walk around. It's a college campus. Turning, I look around the room once again. There's no club, no Benji. I'm... free. I bite my lip in excitement. The chance to mingle with kids my age, find a man to love swirling in the pit of my stomach, I might pee myself with happiness. I look to the mirror on the wall to freshen up before heading out, and can't help but frown at my dark and unapproachable appearance. My blond and pink colored hair, with the dark eyeliner framing my green eyes with splashes of blue around the edges. Grabbing a piece of my hair, I twist it in my fingertips. I've always wanted to change it. I tilt my head to the side.

"New place, new me." I tell my reflection. My small nose wrinkling with excitement.

Papers on the desk next to me flutter to the floor from the breeze of the ceiling fan and I bend down grabbing one.

Professor Michael Prescott Auditorium 1B.

I tap the paper with my black fingernail that's beginning to chip. Harley must have signed up for classes already. Ready to get out and adventure before I lose the light and Harley is back, I toss the paper on the desk and I head out of the dorm room and outside. Kids with bags of all colors and shapes pass by. Cliques sticking close and talking as I wander along the sidewalk, and a couple of jocks toss a football along the green grass. I can't stop from smiling. I'm free, and it feels good.

Looking straight ahead I see a dome building with black bold letters above the door. 1B. That must be where I'm supposed to go. Stepping up the concrete steps, the black boots on my feet feel heavy.

I notice I'm wearing ripped jeans and a black shirt with a leather jacket. Ugh, I'll have to go shopping after this. Harley's clothing is so dark and grim it depresses me.

Once inside the building, it's quiet as everyone has already found seats.

"Do you think Romeo would do it all over again?" a tall man asks the crowd. He has dark short hair and is wearing a white dress shirt with an ugly yellow tie positioned perfectly down the center. His black slacks matching his black shiny shoes peeking out from under his pant legs. His jaw is sharp with a five o'clock shadow, and he has the cutest smile I've ever seen.

"Can I help you?" I jump where I stand, looking around. *Is he talking to me?*

"Miss?"

I look at the professor, and he's looking right at me. Holy crap.

I clear my throat, my skin feeling sweaty. "Is this Professor Prescott's class?" I ask meekly. He smiles, oh God, he smiles handsomely.

"Yes, that's me." He nods.

I step further into the room, not sure where to sit. Do I sit next to someone or should I sit by myself?

"Are you new?"

"I, um?" I begin to doubt being in here. I should turn around. Everyone is looking at me. They have laptops and books. I have nothing.

"Sit here." He points to a chair right in front of his desk. I sigh with relief that he suggested where to sit. Pinching my lips together, my hands squeezing each other I head to the seat. Everyone watches me closely as I step by, and it makes me nervous. I smile politely and head to my seat though.

Slipping into the wooden seat, I look up at him unsure of what to do next. I've never been to a school before.

"Do you have a pencil or anything?" he asks, his light blue-gray eyes looking at me. They look like the sky during a cold rain.

"I don't," I inform with a small smile.

He turns and grabs one off his desk.

"Use mine." He hands me a blue writing utensil. Taking it from him, his fingers brushes mine, and a jolt of electricity circuits through my hand. When he doesn't release his clutch on the pencil my eyes slide to his. They're dancing with hunger, and burning with lust. A handsome smirk crosses his face, and he finally lets go of the pencil. It's not until then that my lungs burn and I realize I'd held my breath the whole time we played tug-o-war with the pencil. Exhaling, I curl my toes and look down with blushing cheeks.

"As I was saying, there's much hidden in the romance of Romeo and Juliet—"

Looking the pencil over I notice Prescott stamped in gold on the side. Teeth marks biting into the wood near the eraser. My fingers rub along the indentions as I silently say his name. His mouth was here, his tongue and saliva on this very pencil.

I bite my lip thinking about him nibbling on the end.

I peek up and catch him staring at me with heated eyes. Blue-gray eyes looking like a hostile storm.

Oh, this is going to be fun.

The Next Day

SITTING in my seat at the top of the auditorium instead of right up front, I wait for Professor Prescott to start class. He's running late today. I feel giddy sitting in my seat, in an actual classroom. I've never attended school before, so this is a whole new scene for me. A tall boy in a letterman's jacket walks past me, grinning from ear to ear. I wink, chewing on the end of my pencil. Butterflies fill my stomach thinking about all the trouble I can get into here. Harley would be pissed.

Harley has no interest in men, boys, anything with a dick. Not that I know of anyway. She is more goal oriented and searching for where she belongs in life.

I know where I belong, in the arms of a man.

I scan the class. People watching. It's something I could do all day. I don't get out much, so it doesn't take much to fascinate me.

I don't understand today's generation. Tattoos claiming every inch of skin. Piercings in every orifice. They are all pretending to be hardcore when in reality, none of them have what it takes. If a gun was pressed to their head, they'd all piss themselves running. Their image is a façade of what lays in their chest. It fascinates me how fake people are. My phone chimes and I look down at it. A missing person's statement. Shrugging, I slide my phone back in my pocket.

Pulling my earbuds out of my bag, I stick them in my ears to tune out the class. Classical music from Beethoven plays on my iPod. Something Harley wouldn't ever listen to and I'm surprised she hasn't delete it off the iPod since I've been gone.

Closing my eyes, I nod my head and tap my pencil against the desktop.

This is my favorite class; Professor Prescott's. He teaches English. I don't care about the lesson. I care about watching him. The way his arm bulges as he writes on the whiteboard. The way he clears his throat and his Adam's apple moves just right against his scruffy throat.

Who cares how much older he is than me, he's divine. He's what you would call white collar, and handsome. Nothing Harley would give a second glance to. Harley is leather and drugs, so naturally, she'd be attracted to that kind of trash.

I'm nudged from the right and my eyes pop open. My head whips to my right with furrowed brows.

The boy sitting next to me juts his chin at the front of the room. Looking forward, I notice the whole class staring at me, and so is Professor Prescott. Class started and I was here having a concert in my head.

My body warms, and I yank my buds out of my ears. My cheeks warming from all the eyes looking at me.

"Harley, see me after class," Professor Prescott snaps. Oh, he's angry. He's even sexier when he's mad.

"Actually, it's Farrah," I correct him. His brows narrow as he slips a piece of paper off his desk, looking at it as if he's missed something. Probably the class roster. "I just, I like to be called Farrah is all," I try and clear up the confusion. Harley signed up for the class, so of course he thinks I'm her. Trying to explain why I'm Farrah and not Harley would scare him more than anything and that's the last thing I want. My thighs squeeze together as everyone stares at me with curious eyes, all the attention has blood racing to my core making me wet.

Everything about me is confusing to a lot of people. I'm not Harley though, I'm Farrah. We are two different people in the same body. I don't get to come out much to play though, as Harley has been very good at keeping me away. She must be on some medication or doing more therapy.

She fucked up being around so much temptation, though. It brought me to the front, and I'm not going away so easily.

"Okay, well see me after class, *Farrah*," he repeats, a dark tone dragging out both syllables of my name. I swallow and nod slowly. He looks up at me and gives me that look again. One of hunger and longing. My thighs clench together at how my name spills from his lips. He's never said *my* name before.

I want to hear it again.

And I will.

———

AFTER PROFESSOR HANDS out the class assignment, I open my laptop I purchased on my handy dandy credit card and start Googling books to read for the project. I feel eyes staring at me and I glance up, catching Professor Prescott looking right at me with heated eyes. I purse my lips trying to keep from smiling and look back at the screen. My chest tightens as I can still feel him staring at me. The hunger in his eyes not unnoticed. We've been playing this cat and mouse game for a couple days now. There's something about him that brings the worst out of me.

I want him so bad. He's all I think about.

Word is he's married. The thrill that he looks at me with such lust even though he's with another woman leaves many questions in my head. Is his marriage bad? Is he in the middle of a divorce?

Who really cares though?

I silently laugh to myself. Harley would never approve, which is why I'm going to fuck him.

The bell rings and the professor stands up.

"Class is dismissed, I will see you all tomorrow." I wait for everyone to leave, my skin ablaze with the knowledge I'll be left alone with the sexy professor. I pull at the thin fabric of the flower dress I'm wearing, trying to cover more of my thighs, but it's not doing much for my modesty with my hard nipples poking through the top.

Bras are overrated.

"Farrah?" he snaps, gesturing for me to come forward. I grab my things and step down to his desk.

"Sorry about the disruption, I was—"

"I would appreciate it if you would be more cautious of our surroundings and be better prepared for my class," he schools, shuffling papers on his desk. He's acting aloof, superior even, and it causes my head to vibrate with confusion. All those looks he's been giving me have been in my head? The pull I feel between us is real. Right? At my uneasiness, anger creeps its way inside my head. I cork a fake smile, knowing if I get too angry Harley will come forward.

The irony of him telling me to be on time for class is cute though.

Noticing my smirk, he does a double take before his face hardens. "Something funny?" His tone harsh, but something I've learned growing up around bikers ... is this man is anything but tough.

"Professor, how can you tell me to be more prepared, when you yourself were late?" I tilt my head to the side, my dark China bangs falling in my face. Sexual tension riles up and laces between us, binding us together in a forbidden atmosphere. It's electric and my nipples ache for him to touch me.

His fiery blue eyes snap to mine, and a cold rush of desire rushes over me, and I have to look away. He's unlike anything I've seen before. He's clean, good, soft hands, and a gentle smile.

I peek back at him. He could be easy to love. I... could be easy to love.

"What I do on my own time is my business, Farrah," he clips. He leans back on his desk, his hands resting on the lip of it, his feet crossed in front of him. The vindication in his voice hangs loosely on his tongue as if he's waiting for me to argue.

He's very unhappy with me, and it whirls a hurricane of guilt in my chest.

"I'm sorry." My smile fades, and I glance down feeling foolish.

Lifting his hand, he tucks one of the strands of hair framing my face behind my ear. My entire right cheek warms with fire from the simple touch. God, I want him to touch more of me.

"Didn't your mother ever tell you not to back talk your elders. That it's bad," he mutters, and the words of manners twist in my stomach like a bad lunch.

Anger boils beneath the surface and the innocent mask begins to slip from my face. I grit my teeth, trying to get a handle on myself. Harley is fighting for the light, I can feel her rattling the cage within, demanding I vanish.

"What can I say, Professor, I guess I'm just a defiant woman." I flirt, sultry hanging off my tongue desperately. I peer up under thick lashes, my lips parting as a harsh breath leaves my mouth. The touch of my skin clearly affecting him, I notice his dick swell in his slacks. I want to ask him if his wife makes him happy? Happy like I know I could. If she fucks him into oblivion? Takes his cock like I would. I want to so bad, but it would be out of line.

I choke out a breath, stuffing down the things I really want to say. Things... much more risqué.

Fire erupts in his eyes, his blue dress shirt stretching with his large inhale. Quickly he turns, his hands still on the desk.

"That will be all," he growls, almost as if he's in pain looking at me. I affect him. Smiling like the devil I am, I hold my books close to my chest and turn on my heel. The cuffs of his dress shirt are rolled to his elbows just enough for me to run my nails over his skin as I walk away and his muscles tense from my touch. Our eyes lock, and the very corner of his lips curves into a smirk.

"See you next time," I whisper, and a playboy smile flashes across his face.

LYING on my bed I stare at the picture of Professor Prescott on the college website. "Michael." My tongue slides along my teeth as I say his name out loud. He's so damn handsome it's almost unfair. I sigh, my nails digging into the skin of my right thigh as I think about what it would be like to have him lying on top of me, or is he the kind that would rather have me on top.

The TV catches my attention and I close the laptop.

If you have any information on the whereabouts of Harley Vander, please call 1800 - Missing.

A picture of a beautiful young woman with long blonde and pink hair with soulless eyes is plastered across the TV screen. Her eyeliner thick and dark, her nose and lip pierced. She's covered in colorful tattoos, too.

Stepping over to the mirror hanging above a cracked sink in the corner, I look at my reflection. My dark brown hair streaked with parts of pink, and lips are stained with pink lipstick from earlier.

I smile like the Devil as I gaze upon myself. They'll never find Harley Vander, not until I say so.

She's not pushing me to the side again, relenting me from coming forth. I'm a part of her, regardless of what she tells herself.

She's the darkness, I'm the light. Without me, she's just a lonely nightmare lost in the atmosphere of reality. She's the rough touch, the misfit of society. I'm the soft caress, the flirty girl next door.

She needs me, otherwise... why would her mind and soul create me?

4

BENJI

TWELVE YEARS OLD

"*Harley, want to go play in the motorcycle graveyard?*" *I ask out of breath, running from the clubhouse. The graveyard is behind the club and is a mountain made up of used motorcycle parts. Harley and I have been trying to piece our own bikes together for a while now, and sometimes when we get bored we pretend to ride the ones that are still half built.*

Harley turns and glares at me. She looks... different. Her hair is cut shorter, and she's wearing a dress. I've never seen her wear a dress before, not since the day I met her.

"*What'd you call me?*" *she sneers, shoving me in the chest hard. Her choppy blonde hair flinging in her face.*

"*Ow,*" *I whine, looking her over in a curious manner. Is she playing a game?*

"*What are you playing?*"

"*Playing? I'm not playing anything,*" *she shrugs, kicking some rocks with high heels that are way too big for her. "Do you want to play spin the bottle?" Her eyes light up, as she holds a dusty beer bottle in her hand.*

I've been trying to accidentally kiss Harley ever since I met her. She made it clear she wasn't ready for that with me or anyone though, so playing a game of spin the bottle is throwing me off. Why now? What's changed?

"Huh? I thought you said you just wanted to be friends?" *I hate myself for reminding her, but I don't want to make her do anything she'd regret. When I kiss her, I want it to be like one of those war-head candies. Explosive at first, leaving her lips tingly and mouth watering for more just before it gets sweet and savory.*

"I'm Farrah, and I'd love to be more than friends." *She holds her hand out, her tone of voice soft and sexy. Farrah? I squint my eyes and tilt my head to the side.*

"Are you sick, Harley?" *I ask, shielding my eyes from the sun. Harley is different today. The way she stands, talks, and looks at me, it's as if someone else is standing before me.*

A voice sounds from behind, a cackle more like it.

"Sick? That girl is a fucking retard. Who does she think she is today? The president, a... a famous singer?" *Prospect Bats laughs, slapping his knee like it's the funniest thing he's ever heard.*

I look back at Harley, who has tear-filled eyes. It twists my chest in a way I feel my ribs might pull apart one by one.

"Don't talk about her that way!" *I shout, stepping in front of her in a protective stance.*

"Oh, give it five minutes, she'll think she's Sara, the gymnast who has cancer," *he throws a hand at me. Waving me off like making fun of Harley is no big deal.*

"Stop calling me names. My name is ..." *she looks down confused and hurt. My chest pulls tightly wanting to protect her. I promised her I'd protect her the day we were both shoved in the back seat of my dad's car together.*

Bending down, I grab a rusty muffler and throw it at Prospect Bats. It strikes him right across the face before skidding across the cigarette butt littered concrete.

"You little Bastard!" *Bats hollers, holding his cut cheek.*

"*RUN!*" *I tell Harley, and we make a bolt for it into the graveyard. From that moment on, I knew Harley would need my protection for the rest of her life.*

I didn't get that first kiss that day, but we never saw Prospect Bats ever again.

5

BENJI

PRESENT

Leaning up against the clubhouse, the desert kicks up in the night's sky, the moon casting shadows on the ground. A lone coyote runs across the way with a rabbit in its mouth, leaving a trail of blood behind it. The sight of it raining crimson into the dirt makes my hands ache. For the rage building inside of me is becoming unbearable. Sitting idle while Harley is missing is not my calling.

Grudge, my president and Harley's father, ordered a missing persons report, and went about his life as usual. As if his duty as a caring father to a sick daughter is done because he had the police station put out a missing person alert. *What the fuck?*

We should be out there ourselves looking, cause we both know ain't no fucking cops out there looking for Harley.

But as his enforcer, I'm supposed to agree with his decision and keep the fuck quiet. I'm not sure how much longer I can uphold that duty.

I was born and raised inside the life of being a biker. The wild lifestyle of being an outlaw is dangerous, and a privilege. Yeah, that's right, a privilege. Not everyone is granted a spot at the table or given a cut with the Shadow Keepers colors. You have to prove that your loyalty to the brotherhood is your only fucking family tree.

The club comes before yourself, before Harley. Grudge says anyway.

I think family should come first, otherwise what the fuck are you trying to protect in the first place.

Taking a drag off my cigarette, I wonder where Harley is. It's all I've thought about since I noticed she wasn't coming back to the club. I checked the roof, the graveyard, everywhere. I'm scared for her. She is strong, but not strong enough. She needs me and she doesn't even fucking know it.

She never has. Friend-zoned and I fucking hate it.

"You all right?"

Glancing to my left, I find Tickles standing outside the club door. Her arms crossed in front of her, pushing her tits nearly out of her top.

I ignore her, exhaling smoke. She's always trying to fuck, but I'm not into sloppy fifteenths.

"You lonely?" she asks, looking out into the night. She has on a jean skirt, and black corset. No shoes. Most of the men in this club have been up in that pussy, but not me. I only have eyes for one wild woman. Harley.

I still ignore Tickles, but she's not one to back down so easily.

"I don't know why you hold out for that bitch. She doesn't give two shits—"

I grab Tickles by the throat before I realize what I'm doing. Shoving her up against the building her eyes widen with fear. She knows she's fucked up now. Nobody speaks ill of Harley. Not around me. Not ever.

"That *bitch* is your club princess, and she is more woman than you'll ever be, Tickles!" I rasp, my grip tightening around her hickey printed throat.

She pinches her eyes shut, her fingers scratching my hand as I take the life from her. I should, I should kill her right here. Make an example to this whole fucking club that Harley is not just a sick girl.

But if I kill this slut, I'd have some horny brothers pissed at me.

I let go, and she doubles over coughing, rubbing her throat.

"She's crazy! She needs to be locked up, Benjamin!" she cries, singing the same tune a lot of people who don't know Harley have sung... Right before me and my close brothers killed them.

I scoff.

"Harley is crazy, but she's original. That's what makes her beautiful." I smile, picturing Harley and her wild spirit as if she was right beside me. She's not what everyone tries to be or thinks they should be. Harley is her own woman and one day... she will be my woman.

She just hasn't seen that yet.

She's making me chase her, and I will.

Grudge named her Harley knowing the day she was born that she would be a free spirit. Untamable.

He didn't know how right he was until she reached puberty. Her dad swore me to stay away from her, and that's the day I fell in love with the forbidden Harley Vander.

Watching Chuckie's Bride, Harley fell asleep in my lap sometime near the end. The weed and whiskey combo too much for her. The club had a party tonight, but her father ordered her to stay in her room this time. Those close to the club know to stay out of Harley's pants, but if Farrah comes out around someone who doesn't know Harley or the club rules... then that's a bloodbath the club doesn't need.

Slowly, I move her head off my lap and kiss her forehead. I couldn't help but stop and really look at her. The lights from the TV flicker across her face, and I slide my finger over her few freckles by her eye. Her skin is soft and silky. My index finger caresses her lips, and I wonder what it would be like to play out one of my many fantasies by slipping the tip of my cock between those angelic lips.

My dick pulses and I realize I'm giving myself blue balls.

Throwing a blanket over her, I step out of her room and gently close the door. The cucumber-scented lotion in my bathroom calling my cock's name.

"Well, well," the familiar slur of my president makes my shoulders tense. I turn, finding Grudge leaning up against the wall, a bottle of whiskey hanging from his right hand. He's trashed.

"It's not what it looks like," I inform, my hands up.

"I don't fucking care to hear it." He stumbles to me, and I lift my chin. My eyes look anywhere but at him, he's a loose cannon when he's drinking. "Stay the fuck away from her, or I will make sure you're a dead boy. You understand?"

My nostrils flare, rage making my hand tighten into a ball. My skull ring digs into my surrounding fingers painfully but I squeeze tighter. The pain makes me focus on it instead of hitting Grudge.

He throws the whiskey bottle at me, liquid splashing on my shirt.

"DO YOU UNDERSTAND!" His face so close he spits in my face.

"I understand!" I holler, my chest bumping into his. Head to head, both of our faces red and determined. Grudge's face grows slack before an arrogant grin tugs at his lips.

"Good boy." He pats my right cheek, before stumbling off to his room. I scowl at him, wanting so badly to beat the fuck out of him. I'm not his fucking dog, and I'll never stay away from Harley. Ever.

Tickles' presence brings me from my memory, and I'm irritated she's still standing there. Flicking my cigarette at Tickles, I head inside and sneak up to Harley's room. Looking for clues as to where she might have been.

Stepping into her room one side is pink and girly, the other side rough and full of club shit. The yellow surfboard is fastened to the ceiling, and a pair of rubber fins are thrown in the corner. I remember when she thought she was a pro surfer. She practiced on the lake thirty miles from here, and she would swear it was the ocean. I took her every day until she fell off her board and cut her leg on a sharp bedrock one evening. I freaked out and nearly drowned myself trying to get to her when she came up screaming.

Sitting on the sand, I toss rocks into the lake while Harley, or should I say, Eden, surfs. The wind is strong today, causing light waves to run across the large lake. The sand is hot, and the sun is causing my nose to redden. I should be on a run with the boys today, Grudge is going to chew my ass out when I get back.

But if I don't watch Harley, who will? I don't trust anyone else to take care of her like I can.

Looking up, Eden loses her balance on the board, her forehead colliding with the fiberglass before falling hard into the water. I stand, my heart stalling.

A small wave washes over where she fell, pushing her board further away.

"Harley?" I wait for her head to pop up. She's been under too long. I tug my leather cut off, and pull my shirt over my head.

An ear-piercing scream echoes amongst the area as Harley's head pops up from the water, a cloud of red drifting around her.

Boots still on, I jump in the water. Moss tangles around my ankle and I jerk as hard as I can to free myself, but all I manage to do is pull myself deeper. I grab my pocket knife from my pocket and slice through the slimy green. Popping to the top of the water I gasp for air.

The sound of Harley sobbing my fuel, I being to swim to her. I grab her, wrapping my arms around her small body and holding her tight.

"What happened?" I ask, tossing my wet hair from my face.

"It's my thigh," she cries, trying to lift it. Looking down all I see is blood. Using my right arm, I swim us to the shore.

Her right tit has fallen from her top, and I can't help but look. Her nipple is so pink, so fucking hard, it takes everything I have to focus on the blood and not fucking Harley into the sand.

"It's right here," she points to her thigh. There's a tip of a rock lodged into her skin. It's deep.

"Don't pull it," I instruct her. "It will make it bleed more. Let's get you to the club doctor, and we will get it stitched up." I scoop her up off the bloody sand, and she clings to my chest.

"Don't forget my board, I'm going to need it," she murmurs. I look over my shoulder, finding the surfboard splashing back and forth with the red waves on the shore.

Blinking away the memory, I look up at the surfboard on her ceiling. You can still see the tinge of red on the tip of it from her blood. Hands on my neck I look around the room, you can see she's not right in the head. There are many things thrown about her room from all of her alters.

It doesn't stop me from wanting to be with her, though.

I don't want someone ordinary, that's not who I am.

Like my father used to say, "Find something you love, and let it kill you."

Harley is my something.

The scent of her cheap bubblegum and the hint of her leather jacket and boots fills her room. It makes me miss her so fucking much. My chest constricts with heartache and rage. I grab the dresser, my fingers digging into the wood. Hollering with fury, I knock her dresser to the floor. Drawers splinter and clothes fling across the room as it breaks. I hate that I love her, I wish for anything in the world I could fucking have a bitch suck my cock, and not close my eyes only to see Harley.

Turning around, I press my hands against the wall and hang my head, my breathing labored.

"Where the fuck are you, Harley?" I whisper in anguish.

If her father won't find her... I will. I'm done waiting around.

"You know, I've watched you sniff around my daughter since I brought her to this club. I told you to keep your little prick to yourself, and we both know you didn't." The voice of Grudge has me tense, but I don't look over my shoulder.

"I don't know what you're talking about," I snarl.

"Seeing you so undone about her disappearance proves to me you can't follow orders, Benjamin. Never have, and never will."

I turn, my face red. His peppered colored hair falls in his face. You can tell the outlaw life has played its toll on the man. That and Harley. "Harley is not well, and without her medicine she is unpredictable and a risk to this club—"

"She's fine. It's people like you that make her feel like she has to run to fucking prove herself!"

I point at him, angry that he talks so ill about her. It makes me question how much he really loves her. I look up at the ceiling. Part of this is my fault, I recited over and over words from Grudge, making Harley run.

"Possibly," he chuckles like tormenting his daughter is funny. He steps into the room and bends over scooping up two orange pill bottles.

"Or maybe it's because she needs to be locked up. You act like an animal, you get treated like one," he states.

My heart seizes and my jaw drops. Harley forgot her fucking medication. Harley is diagnosed with split personality disorder, and who knows what or who she thinks she is right now without her medicine.

"That's rich coming from a man that's the king of killing innocent people." I glare at him. "Look around you, Grudge. We're all fucking animals, otherwise, there would be no Shadow Keepers."

He shrugs, indifferent to my talking back to him. He rubs at his chin casually as he surveys the overturned dresser.

"You might be right," he mutters. "But not knowing what the animal is, is what makes Harley so dangerous. When you look at her, you never know who she is or what she's thinking."

I look down and shake my head.

"You just don't know her like I do," I whisper before looking up at him.

He looks at me, his hand on his chin. "I think we're just

dealing with Farrah this time. The credit card Farrah normally uses has recently been used online," Grudge informs. Harley doesn't use her credit card for anything, so when it's used... it's usually when she loses control and Farrah has emerged from the depths of Harley's soul. Harley has had many personalities come and go since I've known her but Farrah has been there since the day I've met her. Farrah is the most unpredictable of her personalities too. She's always coming and going, and I get a sense she doesn't care about what Harley wants.

Fucking Farrah is like fucking for the first time, every time.

I try to love Farrah as much as Harley, but Farrah insists I'm not her type. However, that hasn't stopped us from fucking every time she comes forth. My cock keeps her thirst for love satisfied.

The best way to describe Farrah is a confused girl looking for love. Carrie with blood spilled down her beautiful dress on prom night as her heart breaks at her feet. She'll do anything for love, even if it means ruining Harley to get it. Unlike Farrah who uses her charm and seductive body to get her way, Harley uses a sharp tongue and violence. That's why I love her.

She's a sexy grenade.

"Yeah... I should have just put her in a mental hospital. She'd be safer," he mumbles, looking at the pill bottles. I grind my teeth thinking about him turning his back on her. She's not the easiest person to love, but sometimes the hardest thing and the right thing are unavoidable.

Harley is unavoidable.

I step over to him, my mind racing with what the hell Harley or Farrah might be facing out there. The fact that Harley might come too and be lost, or hurt, making me white-knuckle my rage.

His cold eyes drop to my face, his thin lips tugging into a tight smirk. He knows I'm at my breaking point, and he also knows if I touch him... the entire club could retaliate against me.

"She's your daughter, our princess. If she's hurt, you're risking your position at the head of our table," I threaten him.

His brows furrow.

"You want to be the president of this fucking club, son?" His question sounding more of a joke, but the tension in his stance tells me otherwise. I never thought about taking that gavel, but the way our club is in debt and the way Grudge turns his back so quickly on what is ours... taking over might be where I'm needed to keep this club alive.

Grudge forces out a chuckle, an attempt to lighten the mood.

"Yeah, well, until then you can be my errand boy." He insults.

He opens his palm offering me the pill bottles. I flick my gaze to him.

"Find her and bring her back. Quietly." His demand is laced with a silent warning. One that if I don't obey orders... I'll pay the price. Or Harley will. I still remember the day his loving father act died, and it was just me defending Harley.

I search behind the old Rat Rod parked behind the garage when I see her behind the large tire. She's naked, covered in blood, and shivering.

"Harley?"

"Benjamin?" Her chin lifts and her weepy eyes meet mine.

"Why are you hiding? And naked?" On all fours, she crawls to me. Tugging on my shirt, she makes me lower to her level.

"I don't know what happened, Benji, but I think Daddy did something really bad," she whispers, her eyes filling with tears again. Squatting to the oil-stained concrete, I notice her clothes piled in the corner. I take my leather jacket off and place it on her shoulders to cover her body.

"What do you mean?"

"I mean, everyone was on a run and Dad thought I was in my room. I came downstairs and saw him and Buddy fighting. A plant was thrown, and Daddy aimed a gun. One of the club girls ran out of a room naked. Everything went black, and the next thing I know I was standing in a puddle of blood and Dad was dragging a body out the

back door." Her eyes bounce back and forth, her body trembling with fear.

My eyes widen. Grudge can't kill another member without a club vote! We might live off the grid by our own way of life, but we do have rules.

"Are you sure?"

"I don't know, I blacked out again," she cries, her fingers strained in explanation. Her accusing her father of killing a patched-in member is serious business. It means he's gone rogue. She could lose her dad.

I pull her to me, and she clutches my shirt trying to climb onto my lap. I let her, wrapping my arms around her. Making her feel safe.

"Harley, you cannot tell anyone what you saw. Do you understand me?"

I feel her nod, but she doesn't say anything. She saw something she shouldn't have that night, and if Grudge wanted to... he can take her from me to make sure she never spoke of it.

"Chances are the longer I let her run loose out there, the more she puts me at risk." My eyes snap to his, the memory fading. He killed Buddy and Totty that day but acted like they went on a side job and went missing. He made it look like they were killed by a rival club, but me and Harley know what happened. He knows Harley knows what happened.

That is why he hides Harley up here, if anyone knew... he'd be disbanded from the club. Buddy was the club's pot grower, and Totty was a club whore. I know Grudge wasn't happy with Buddy raising prices on the crops, but it was because he had been mixing strains and growing some new shit.

Apparently, a deal went south, and Buddy paid the price. Totty was just in the wrong place at the wrong time. So was Harley.

I snatch the orange containers from his hand and he grabs hold of my wrist before letting me walk away.

"Find her, bring her back." His nostrils flare, his words clipped and angry.

I obey my president in all things club related, but when it comes to Harley... I've never been one to walk the line. I jerk my hand free and glare at him.

"We'll see," I growl. I'm done taking orders from him.

Maybe Harley and I should just run.

6

FARRAH

Standing in line at the coffee shop the overhead air conditioning causes my yellow sundress to tickle my thighs. I brush my bangs from my eyes and tighten my ponytail as I look at the menu above the coffee register when I'm suddenly bumped into from behind. Shoved into once again, I turn, irritated. I swear this campus has no manners.

A young man wearing a beanie with shaggy hair curling out from underneath looks back at me with dazed eyes. He shrugs as if bumping into me is no big deal, his lips move but I can't hear him with my earbuds in. He's probably apologizing. I just nod and turn back around. "Time To Say Goodbye" by Bocelli eases me into the morning hours. My sweaty fingers fumble the change in my hand and I drop the three bucks for my iced coffee. It's going to be one of those days. Bending down, I pick up the money, not realizing my dress rises just a little too far when I hunch over. An earbud falls from my left ear when my head lolls forward.

"I could fuck that ass."

"You couldn't handle anal, you'd blow your load in like five seconds."

My lips purse from the lewd comments, anger boiling within me so hot I begin to flush. I feel humiliated and slutty. Getting me up the ass is not romantic in the least. My vision wobbles as I feel Harley's rage bubbling inside of me. If she comes forward, there's going to be a gruesome scene in this coffee shop.

"Be a man and look away," the familiar sound of Professor Prescott sounds, and my fury instantly dissolves into a puddle of desire. My hero.

Tucking my bottom lip in between my teeth I stand straight and turn around finding professor Prescott with a cup of coffee in his hand. He's freshly showered, his hair slicked back and wet, the smell of spice overtaking the coffee shop.

"Mr. Prescott," I smile, pulling the other earbud from my ear so I can hear everything he has to say. I wouldn't want to miss a word. I blush, and my skin tingles seeing him defend my honor. He stands at least a foot above me, and his strong hand curled around that cup with a death grip.

"Class starts in fifteen minutes, don't be late," he smiles. Bringing his coffee cup to his mouth, his lips curl over the black lid. His Adam's apple bobbing as he takes a small sip. Who knew taking a sip of coffee could make a girl wet?

I tilt my head to the side and wonder if he was being a man and looked the other way like he told those boys to do, or if he was thinking the same thing about my ass.

"Like you wouldn't want to hold me after class again?" I reply sultry, and his eyes become ablaze. We stare at each other, our minds silently playing out what he would do with me if I was his naughty student. He wants me, I can see it not only in his eyes but the way he acts. The way his mouth tugs at the corner in an attempt not to smile when he sees me. The hunger in his eyes when they go heavy with lust when our eyes meet.

"I will see you in class, Farrah." His smile now tight-lipped, he tries to avoid eye contact. His face not giving anything away as he leaves the coffee shop. He can try to act like he's unaffected by me, but it's too late for that, he's already revealed he wants me.

I bite my bottom lip, and the line to the register moves forward. Smiling like a school girl with a crush, I step forward leaving Mr. Prescott with a string of dirty thoughts in his head.

"LET'S TALK ABOUT POEMS," Professor Prescott addresses the class. "Anybody have a favorite from last night's read?" he prods the class, but everyone is quiet. I forgot to read last night's assignment. I was too busy eye fucking the teacher's profile on the campus website. Again

His eyes fall upon mine, and I suck in a tight breath. He's going to call on me, I can feel it.

"Farrah?" he says my name. Not Harley's, but mine. My heart flutters in my chest, and my eyes become hooded as we stare at one another longer than acceptable for teacher and student.

"What was your favorite, Farrah?"

I shrug, twirling my blue pencil along the desktop. Homework, who knew that was really a thing. Maybe he will keep me after and tutor me, but really, we can sit close to each other and get to know one another on a personal level. Stolen glances, soft touches, subtle kisses... sigh.

"Did *anyone* read last night's assignments?" he asks angrily. His arms outstretched as he looks about the room. I clear my throat and sit up looking around the crowd. Seems I'm not the only one who didn't do homework.

"No way man, Alpha PI had the sickest party!" a dumb frat boy replies from the front row, and a bunch of people cheer and holler. Professor Prescott sighs before looking at the clock.

"Class dismissed," he informs irritated before sitting behind his desk.

Everyone leaves, but me. I'm drawn to this man. It's forbidden but exciting. Benjamin and I are not together, no matter what he tells everyone. We've slept together a few times because he has this thing about him I just can't walk away from. Maybe it's his arrogant personality or his persistent chasing after me that has me giving in to him. Deep down though, I think he loves Harley - not me. Besides, he's very controlling and looks like an outlaw. Being away from him, I want to play the field. See a different dick, hear the sound of another man orgasm. Will it be quiet, or loud? Will his cock be smaller or bigger than Benji's?

My mind reels with thoughts of passionate sex now, my fingers flexed upon my pencil so hard, I nearly break it in two.

After the last student leaves, he glances up giving me a double take. He didn't know I stayed behind.

"Can I help you with something?" he questions in that teacher tone. It makes the heat in my cheeks fade.

I stand from my desk and step down to him. Placing my hands on the front of his desk I lean over, the front of my dress drooping and showing my bare breasts.

His eyes catch sight of the loose fabric and my nipples ache watching him stare. I press my dress to my chest and stand upright. The room fills with sexual tension and I clear my throat.

"Did you attend this party everyone went to last night?" he asks, looking down at some papers. A red pen in his hand. He almost sounds jealous.

"Why?"

"It would explain why you couldn't tell me anything about poems today," he replies in a fatherly manner.

"Is having fun a crime? You're not that old are you?" I joke with a roll of my eyes.

He stands abruptly, some papers falling to the floor. This catches my attention, I've never seen him move so swiftly before.

My mouth parts as he steps around the desk and behind me. My heart slamming in my chest, my eyes flutter with longing. As if he read my mind, he grips me by the ponytail, wrapping it around his hand for control. Using his free hand, he shoves me forward causing me to bend over his desk. My dress rising to my ass cheeks, showcasing my flower panties.

I can't breathe, I'm on fire. My panties soaking wet, and my sex pulsing with eagerness.

Weight presses along my back from his body, he brushes his lips along the shell of my ear. Closing my eyes, I can't help the whimper that falls from my sinful lips.

"Do you like this? Is this what you want?" he growls. "Do you want me to fuck you up the ass with my big cock?" His knees press into my thighs keeping me in place, and my nails scratch into the wooden desk with desire. I was wrong, hearing him want to take me up the ass is more than romantic... it's fucking erotic!

He jerks me by the ponytail, my neck arched back as far as it will go. It aches, and I swear it's about to snap, but I don't say anything because if he let go it would be the biggest disappointment. Who knew he was so dominant and aggressive when he's turned on. I want to play with him.

"Yes, do it," I moan. His hard-on presses against my backside, and my body pushes against it. The friction causing me to buck against him on its own free will.

He suddenly pulls away from me, and a cold void wafts around my body. Leaving a chill amongst my heated skin. I look over my shoulder with hooded eyes, my face contorting into embarrassment.

"What's wrong?" I ask breathily.

"I'm married, Farrah." He closes his eyes, hesitation thick in his voice. Rejection plummets in my stomach, coiling my emotions to the point I want to scream in a rage so powerful the windows burst.

"Happily?" I swallow hard. Who cares if he's married, the question is does he care about her?

His hard eyes hit mine.

"Hell no. In fact, I wouldn't be with her if it weren't for her father," he belittles his wife. His face turning a red shade.

"What do you mean?" I ask softly. Was he forced to marry? I don't understand why someone would stay in a marriage if they didn't want to be married.

Rubbing his chin, he shakes his head.

"Sometimes... you don't get to pick who your partner is. June was amazing when I met her, but then she turned into a cold-hearted bitch. She doesn't care about my needs, only her own. She's materialistic, and I'm not. I need something on a more personal level," he explains. "I don't love her, I'm just with her because it's easier than trying to divorce her. Her dad is the fucking governor, after all."

He said it, he doesn't love her. I have to bite my cheek to keep from smiling like an idiot. That means there's a chance he could love me. Maybe if we are meant to be together, he'll even leave her one day.

With the Shadow Keepers behind my back, we could take out the governor and be really happy.

Just as I'm about to nod in understanding, he reaches out and palms me by the face harshly, pulling me into him. His touch hard and controlling. His eyes full of lust and want. The battle of what he wants and what is right storms in his eyes.

Closing my eyes, I lean into his touch for more.

"Fuck it!" he breathes heavily. His breath smelling of coffee.

His lips crash onto mine, and I sigh into him. His tongue seeking mine like a hunter in the Amazon. Using his body, he pushes me backward. My feet stumbling with every step until the back of my thighs hit the front of his desk. He grabs me under the thighs and lifts me, throwing me on top.

My dress rises as I slide along the cold desk.

I palm his smooth cheeks as his lips continue to kiss and peck the sensitive skin of my neck. It's as if he can't taste me enough.

Tilting my head back, I close my eyes and get lost in his touch. It's so sensual and intimate.

"Little girls like boys," echoes in my head. I close my eyes not sure where the memory came from.

"Michael?" a feminine voice catches mine and his attention from the top of the auditorium.

Michael's eyes widen as if he just heard a ghost. He grabs some papers by my thighs, his mood suddenly cavalier. As if he wasn't just tasting me, he pretends to shuffle the papers. Swallowing down my arousal, I quickly slide off the desk to my feet.

My eyes climb the room finding a woman in a long white dress and big sun hat. Big black glasses cover her face, concealing everything but her snooty nose.

"That will be all, Farrah," Professor Prescott dismisses me coldly, and my heart twists until it nearly breaks.

Clearing my throat, I slide my hands down my dress and give a curt nod.

"Who is this, dear?" The lady asks, swiping her glasses off her face. *Dear?*

"Farrah, this is my wife, June," Professor introduces us. "She does counseling for some of the students on campus."

I may vomit. This is the wife.

She holds her hand out, a tight-lipped smile attempting her hard face.

"The governor's daughter to be exact." She tilts her head to the side without a hint of modesty as if her social status means something to me. "You should come see me some time," her eyes squint as she sizes me up. There's more to her offer though, I can see the pique in her eyes. She wants to toy with me behind closed doors. She's unaware that I'll be the cat and she'll be the mouse in this game.

"Oh, Mrs. Prescott. I'm beyond saving," I whisper huskily. She purses her lips, her brows narrowing in. Her eyes flash with admiration before turning into a glare.

"Excuse me, I'm late for my next class," I lie. I just need out of here. My head is swirling with so many thoughts, so many actions, if I don't leave now I'll lose control.

I step past her, but not before looking over my shoulder at the Professor.

He said he didn't love her, hopefully he's not just leading me on to get in my pants.

Because I'll kill him.

7

HARLEY

SIXTEEN YEARS OLD

"Harley, can you tell me why you're here?" I peer through my bangs, a woman sitting in a chair across from me looks at me skeptically. She has brown and gray hair braided into a mess on her head. Wrinkles under her eyes, and she's wearing a white V-neck, and white pants.

She looks like a doctor of some kind.

I look around the room curious how I got here. Last thing I remember was being at the gas station with Viper and Benjamin.

"Where am I?" I ask, my lips trembling with confusion.

"Harley? Can you remember anything?" she asks, her head tilted down as she assesses me. I shake my head, my breathing labored as I look around the room. My head hurts, and my vision blurs from the blood racing through my limbs so quickly.

There's a bunch of windows on one side of the room, and the other side is covered in posters about not giving up, and yoga positions to help with anxiety. Am I in therapy? A hospital?

I look down at my nails scratching into the wooden arms of the chair anxiously. Red stains the cracks of my nails and I furrow my brows. I bring my fingers closer, the smell of metallic lacing up my nostrils and breathing sin into my lungs. It's blood.

My eyes widen into saucers. *Where did I get blood on my hands from?*

"Do you remember hurting anyone?" the doctor asks.

My head snaps in her direction. My eyes filling with tears as my lungs burn for air.

I look at the lady like she's lost her mind.

"Hurt? *I* hurt someone?" I question, a tear slipping down my face. I would remember hurting someone, and I didn't.

She sighs, setting her things on her desk before sitting on the edge of her seat.

"You were at a gas station with your dad and some friends..."

"Benjamin... I remember him being there, and Viper. We went on a beer run for the club and Viper was inside buying cigarettes with Benjamin," I explain, but that's all I remember. Everything after that is a vision of darkness.

"A woman bumped into you and spilled a slushy or some kind of drink on your feet, do you remember that?" I don't reply because I don't remember that happening at all. I look down at my feet and see a sticky residue all over my black boots. When did I put those on? "There were some words spoken, and you grabbed a beer bottle from the case Benjamin was carrying and... well, you broke it and stabbed the woman."

My eyes flutter as my hands try and smother the gasp spilling from my mouth. I stabbed someone with a beer bottle? That doesn't even sound like something I would do.

"No, I didn't do that. I would remember." I shake my head, my world crashing around my feet. They must have the wrong person.

"Do you black out often?" She continues with squinted eyes.

I can't breathe, let alone speak so I just nod in reply. My life bleeds from blackout to blackout. I wake up in odd places, around people I don't know.

"I see. Do you know anyone named Farrah?"

I lift my head slowly from my palms. She said my name. *How does she know my name?*

"I'm Farrah," I whisper confused. See they do have the wrong person.

"I see, and are you aware of Harley then?"

"Who?"

"Farrah, you have a disorder called Dissociative Identity Disorder—"

"What is that?" I sneer, anger pummeling through me like a hot knife.

"It's where, well, multiple people live within you, or Harley. I'm not sure which one of you is in control as I've just met you."

"That's... that's insane." I shake my head. None of this is making sense, I've never even heard of that disorder before. It can't be real. This is a nightmare, it has to be. I grab my arm and pinch the skin between my nails, I feel the pain and I'm still here. In this confusing, scary scenario.

"It's a lot more common than people think. It usually happens from trauma, or an abusive past, it's a coping mechanism. Has anyone hurt you or Harley before?"

"STOP CALLING ME THAT!" I scream with tears raining down my cheeks. She jumps from my outburst, but I continue to stare at her with hostile eyes.

I'm so sick of people calling me Harley. We're different people, with different lives. No wonder they think I killed someone, they think I'm Harley. God, what has she fucking done this time?

Clearing her throat, she settles herself back into her leather chair as if I didn't just scream at her.

"It's common for you and Harley not to be aware of each-other—"

"I know of her, I'm just not her!"

"I see." She writes things down on a notepad, and I feel like I'm being judged.

"Where is Benjamin?" I demand. I can't take this anymore. I look around me, thinking of running out of here. I didn't hurt anyone, I shouldn't be in here.

"Tell me, Farrah, where is your family? Who is Benjamin?"

Closing my eyes, I breathe through her questions.

"My family is gone. A club adopted me, and Benjamin is, I don't know... a friend," I reply with a shaky voice. *What is Benji to me?* I've never had someone ask me that before. He's... always there for me. He's like a brother.

"So, you and Harley are different people?"

My head throbs, my vision funneling in on the stupid doctor in the chair. What does she mean different people. Can she not tell I'm different, that I'm not Harley? Is she not listening?

"I WANT Benjamin!" I scream, done with these stupid questions. Done with her.

The lady sighs. "I'll go get him if it will make you calm down—"

"BENJAMIN!" I scream so loud my face turns red, my heart pounding in my ears to the point all I hear is ringing.

The lady quickly stands and leaves the room with haste. I sit back in the chair, close my eyes and try hard to remember what happened.

But all I see is black. The depths of hell burning fire and ash as I press my fingers into my eye sockets.

"What is wrong with me?"

8

BENJI

G rudge holds me back as I hear Harley scream from the room.

"She's fine, let them do their job, son!" he breathes into the back of my head.

Closing my eyes, all I see is Harley covered in blood with a shocked look on her face. A young woman with short red hair bleeding out on the parking lot from Harley slicing her across the chest.

The door finally opens to her room, and I feel like I can breathe again. The doctor steps out and swallows before speaking.

"She insists her name is Farrah, and is really confused. To be honest, I'm not sure who I was talking to in there, but I'm almost positive she has Dissociative Identity Disorder—"

"What the fuck is that?" Grudge asks almost as if he was insulted. The lady pulls a pamphlet from the wall next to us and hands it to him. The whole wall is littered with pamphlets of different mental disabilities. Glancing over Grudge's shoulder, I see something about multiple personalities or some shit.

My jaw ticks as I think back about how Harley has pretended

to be other people since we've known each other. Farrah has been one of them on numerous occasions. Her dad and I knew she was different, we just didn't know it had a name. That there were other people with the same condition.

"She wants to see you." The doctor looks directly at me with a pointed look.

Pushing past her and Grudge, I rush to Harley before her father can stop me.

Stepping inside the room carefully, Harley is standing in the middle of the room, her body shaking.

"Babe?" I ask cautiously.

She turns, makeup smeared around her eyes from crying.

"Where am I? Am I going to jail, Benji?" she mutters, her face hard and cold. She doesn't have panic in her eyes like before, and she doesn't seem to be scared.

"Harley?" I ask.

She rushes to me and hugs me so tight I never want her to let go.

"I just snapped, I couldn't hold it back," she cries in explanation. I pull her head into my chest. "I think I might be sick, Benji," she whispers. "They're going to take me away."

"It's okay. I won't let anyone take you from me," I mumble into the top of her head.

9

BENJI

Present

"We got word of where Harley is." Viper walks out of the clubhouse, lighting a cigarette. I toss my bag in the back of my El Camino parked right in front of the club. I decided against my motorcycle just in case I need to clean up a mess or bring Farrah back hogtied. "You going to spit it out, Viper?" I scowl. Viper is my best friend. My brother regardless of our DNA or brotherhood. He knows how much I care for Harley, in fact, he's the only one who knows how bad I got it. I broke his nose to be exact.

One night Farrah came forward, and Viper was new to the club. He was just about to be patched-in from prospect. She started flirting with him and when Viper hooked his arm around her waist with that fucking playboy look on his face. I lost all control. I took him to the ground and punched him in the nose until it broke.

That's when he learned about Harley and her sickness, and with a blood-stained rag against his face he told me, "You're lucky I like you, or I wouldn't have let you kick my ass."

We became instant friends, and he's been behind me in protecting Harley ever since.

"A club called the Bastard Makers has a son attending the college, said he saw a girl that looks like Harley but with dark hair. She had your ring on her finger though." Viper runs his hands through his dirty blond hair.

My skull ring, Harley wanted to wear it and it got stuck on her thumb. She's had it ever since.

Her credit card was swiped at Best Buy near the college too, I was going to go look around the area but now that I know exactly where to go, that makes finding her a lot easier.

"Why would she go to a college?" I ask with a frown. I know she's always wanted to go to school, but she's always been hell-bent on being a part of the club, that's what she was upset about when she left.

"The governor's daughter volunteers there," he answers grimly. Our eyes lock, she's not there for school, she's on a mission.

"Fuck, she knows about him owing us money. I was right, she's trying to prove herself to the club." Tight-lipped, I slam my fist into the side of my car. The black paint dents from the impact, and I shake my hand out. The pain pulsing through my knuckles. If she fucks up, the governor could have her killed.

"She's there to grab that bitch, isn't she?" Viper puts two and two together.

"Yeah, or his son-in-law. He teaches there too doesn't he?" I look to Viper.

"Yeah, he does. You think Farrah will fuck him?" he asks.

My neck cracks with that question. I can't even begin to think about that.

"I don't fucking know, but standing here talking to you ain't going to find her." Stepping past him, I jerk the door open to my car and slide in behind the wheel.

"You couldn't find some bitch with a drug habit or a slutty

stripper with two kids? You had to fall head over fucking heels for the female version of Jekyll and Hyde." He shakes his head, an arrogant smile on his face.

"Fuck you. Wait 'til you come across a woman that has you doing the chasing for once. It'll make you see things differently."

He chuckles, blowing smoke into the wind. "Pretty sure it doesn't matter, they're all fucking crazy at the end of the day." If I wasn't so scared for Harley right now, I'd laugh in agreement. "You want me to go with you?" he asks, hovering over my window, a cigarette hanging out of his mouth with ashes about to spill into my lap.

Starting my old car, I shake my head. "No, I can take care of her." I always have. Let's just hope Farrah hasn't opened her fucking legs to some college prick... because that's one thing I can't handle.

I'll lose my shit and the dead bodies will stack up.

She's my disaster, and I'll be damned if I let anyone walk in the wake of my club's princess except me.

10

BENJI

EIGHTEEN YEARS OLD

"Benji, I know we're just friends, and if you want to say no I completely understand. It's just that, I don't know anyone else, and with me being... different—"

"Spit it out, Harley," I laugh, swiping the bottle of Jack we stole from the club from her hand. She jumps down off the mound of parts thrown out by the brothers in the biker graveyard. Mine and Harley's usual go-to for a chance at freedom.

She runs the back of her hand along her forehead as she stares out into the night. Goddamn, she's beautiful. She has a ripped tank top on tonight, showing off her belly button ring and cut off shorts that are two sizes too big, making my mind run wild with what I could do to those exposed hips. I've always loved Harley, but she friend-zoned me. There's nothing worse than wanting to fall to your knees for a women, who only see's you as a friend.

"I want to have sex," she blurts out. Mouth full of Jack, I freeze. Surely, I didn't hear her right.

I swallow the liquid fire. "Sex?" I confirm.

"Yeah, with you." She kicks at a few bolts laying around on the ground. "I've seen it enough around the club, and it scares me that one day... Farrah is going to take the choice away from me." I grit my teeth thinking that her split personality takes away a lot of her life. "You've been with girls before, so you know what you're doing." She shrugs innocently. I actually haven't been with any girl, but Harley doesn't know that. She thinks I've been with tons because I tell her I have. It makes me feel better to throw it in her face because she won't let me have her. I could easily be with the girls around the club, but I want only Harley. The forbidden flower inside my own club.

"Yeah, I mean. If you're sure." I try to play it cool, but my dick is so hard I can feel the veins in my shaft throbbing.

Her eyes shoot to mine, her teeth nibbling on her bottom lip.

"Yeah?" the question falls from her mouth so perfectly, it has me drop the bottle of jack to the ground, and slide off the mound of bike parts a little too eagerly.

Quickly I make my way to her. My hands hesitating before falling to her bare hips. Goddamn her skin is so soft, like fucking silk. I feel high, my body vibrating as I touch her bare skin. I want to fuck her bad, so fast but slow at the same time, my mind is racing with what to do.

She places both of her hands on my chest, her eyes closed.

"If I say stop... you'll stop?" She looks up at me with doe eyes.

"Of course," I whisper. But honestly, I've wanted this so long... I'll never stop. I'm slamming my dick in that pussy and placing my claim on her before anyone in this fucking world can.

Pushing up on her tiptoes she closes her eyes, her lips pursing. Grabbing the nape of her neck with one hand, the other grasping her left hip, I pull her close and press my mouth to hers.

I want to be everything a first time should be for a girl like her deserves. But I'm going to show her I'm no fucking friend...

I demand her lips apart, and I take what I've been longing for, for far too long. Our kiss is rough, greedy, wet, and goddamn perfect. Her mouth tastes of cheap bubblegum and I can't get enough of it. She's always leaving Double Bubble wrappers around the club, and I've come to love the smell.

She's a curse and a blessing. Wild, but caged inside of her own mind.

My hands slide up her soft curves, and her head falls back as she offers herself to me like a lamb to a wolf. Under her shirt, I grasp her bare breast, her pebbled nipple pressing into my hand. The feel of them in my callused palm.

"Fucking perfect," I groan. Pushing my hand along her spine, her body bends just right and I lower my head. I flick her nipple with my tongue, swirling it in my mouth before nipping it gently.

"Oh God," she mews.

One hand on each of my cheeks, she looks up at me with glossy eyes.

"I've wanted this for so fucking long," I confess, kissing her tit.

Her eyes widen like this is news to her.

"Fuck me, Benji. Fuck me like one of your club whores."

Snapping upright, I fist her hair.

"I'll fuck you, but I'll never disrespect you like a club whore. Do you understand?"

Her lashes flutter before she nods softly.

Lacing my palm with hers, I lower her to the dusty ground, my knees straddling her body. The mounds of used parts and broken motorcycles from over the years conceal us from everyone at the club. It's just me and Harley. She looks up at me with scared eyes, not sure what to do next.

I take charge, leading the way.

My fingers hook into each side of her shorts and pull them down her thighs. Her arousal drips from her pussy making it glisten against the moonlight. Woman walk around the club naked, but I've never had a cunt this close up before.

I inhale a deep breath, the smell of Harley turning me on even more. I knew she didn't wear panties. One day when she had on some baggy sweatpants with holes in them, I swear I saw pink pussy when she was sitting on the couch. She's wild, free, and mine tonight.

Using the pad of my finger, I slide it through her wet lips and her body arches as if a jolt of electricity circuited through her limbs.

Leaning over her, I kiss her, taking her moans and pleasure. My elbow pressed into the hard ground I jerk my baggy jeans down to my knees. My dick falls free, brushing against the ground.

"I want to see," she presses on my chest, her eyes narrowed in the direction of my hard-on.

Using my knees, I sit up, and my hard cock throbs as she looks at it with curious eyes.

Her fingers reach out, her fingertip slightly caressing the tip of my cock. My dick jumps, and she startles.

What can I say, my cock knows who it wants, and it's been wanting Harley since before I learned how to jack off.

My balls squeeze, needing to be inside of her. Now.

"Show and tell is over," I rasp.

I push her back down onto the ground and push her knees as far apart as I can.

Her eyes widen by my sudden control.

Fisting the base of my cock I press it against her entrance. Her eyes locked on mine, and I slowly push myself into her tightness.

Oh my God, it feels so fucking good. She's so warm, so wet, I push further inside.

Her mouth parts, her eyes furrowing with unease.

She whimpers, and my restraint busts. I thrust into her a little harder.

She envelops around me, her body tense. I make myself slow down, letting her adjust to my size.

"You okay?" I whisper into her ear. The intense tingling in my cock causing my hips to rock on their own. I can't stop, I knew I couldn't once I was inside of her.

Breathing heavily, she nods, and slowly she untangles herself from my chest and lays herself back on the ground.

Tucking my hand behind her neck, I work myself deeper and deeper inside of her. Glancing between our bodies, I notice her tits are beading with sweat, her flat stomach breathing heavily. Fuck she's beautiful. I've envisioned this moment for so fucking long.

My hips have a mind of their own they circle, thrust, and drown in pure fucking satisfaction as I fuck her.

Her tongue snakes out, sliding along her bottom lip as she looks up at me with pleasure instead of fear now.

I give a chaste kiss against her damp lips, and her teeth graze the skin of my lip. She's getting brave.

I'm fucking done trying to be a gentleman now.

"Widen your legs more." My voice raspy, and her legs outstretched causing my cock to sink further inside of her. I want to pound into her so hard, feel her come undone and whimper from the power of my cock.

My balls squeeze with warmth and my face masks with pleasure.

"I'm going to come," I warn her. I don't want it to end, I want to keep going but the release is too great. I can't stop it.

"Do it inside of me," she pants. My eyes widen.

"You on the pill?" I ask, not wanting to fuck both of our lives up.

She nods impatiently.

Fisting her tit harder than I should, I tuck my face inside of her neck. I lick the salty sweat from her skin, and just as I feel the first drop of cum slip from the tip of my dick. I suck on her collarbone and blow my load inside of her sweet cunt. Grunting, my boots scuff against the dirt trying to find purchase as I drive into her over and over. The burn on my knees from the hard ground going unnoticed as I fuck Harley in the motorcycle graveyard.

I'm pissed it's over and pleased I marked her as my first. My chest battles the emotions. Am I happy or mad?

Out of breath, I slowly pull from her tightness, only it's not nearly as tight as when I first entered her. The sight of blood stains my dick and the lips of her pussy. I can't help but smile that I took her virginity.

I fall next to her and we both look up at the stars. Her thighs and pussy covered in blood, and my pants around my ankles.

"Will it always hurt like that?" she asks calmly. The sound of her voice back in a friendly matter, and not in a lusty tone like it was.

"No, it will get better each time you do it," I inform her. But I'll never let her fuck another man, not while I'm still breathing.

"It was like, kissing with your whole body," she whispers. I look to her watching the stars with glossy eyes and red cheeks. A simple smile playing across her swollen lips. Having Harley tonight, it's made me realize just how fucking amazing Harley really is.

I push a strand of hair from her face, and she grabs my hand. Her little fingers twisting my skull ring off my finger. She places it on her index finger and it falls off. Lost in her own world, she places it on her thumb. It's a perfect fit.

She smiles, holding it above her head like it's a diamond ring.

"HARLEY!" Grudge yells for her. We both look in the direction of the club. If her dad catches us, I'll be pistol whipped and Harley will be locked in her room for days.

"Shit, I better go," she whispers. Standing, she pulls her shorts up and straightens herself. She tosses her hair over her shoulder and looks at me.

Pulling my jeans up I step up to her, grabbing her hand before she runs away.

"I don't want things to get weird between us, Harley," I beg her. As much as I wanted this, it wouldn't be worth losing her.

She smirks, dimples forming on each side of her swollen lips.

"Don't worry, we will always be best friends."

Like a fucking knife to the chest, I let go of her hand. I was hoping she would be like most chicks after me fucking her and feel like we had something special or some shit. But she's Harley, she's not any ordinary girl. She turns to run off to the club but stops.

"Your ring!" she whispers. She tugs and pulls on the ring on her thumb, but it doesn't budge. Worried eyes look at me.

"I'll get it later, just go!"

She nods and returns to the club, leaving me outside with a lone wolf crying into the night. My chest pounds with disappointment, and it makes me angry I feel this drawn to her.

I don't want to be her friend.

I want to be her fucking man.

"Find something you love, and let it kill you," I whisper my dad's advice to no one.

11

PRESENT

FARRAH

Sitting in Professor Prescott's class which I'm surely failing because I don't do homework, I watch him pace back and forth as he lectures the class about Hamlet. I'm sitting in the front row this time, wanting to be near him. His white dress shirt fits his hard chest perfectly today, and black slacks wrap around his ass. He's perfection.

He stops walking, his eyes falling on mine and that handsome white smile flashes my way. I come to life when he looks at me like that. The look of want and desire floating in his eyes making me feel alive.

Butterflies swarm my lower half and I slowly slump down in my seat and widen my legs. He loses his train of thought and stops talking mid-sentence as he eyes fall between my legs. The class waiting for his next words, I look around to make sure nobody is looking at me; they're not. I walk my fingers up my warm thigh and slip them under my pretty panties. My mouth parts as they slide into my wetness and the marker in his hands breaks, spraying ink all over his shirt.

"Fuck!" He drops the marker to the ground. Giggling like a school girl, I pull my hand out from my panties and push my dress back down. He looks at me with heated eyes and a massive bulge in his slacks. I hold up my index finger and lick my juices like a lollipop. I notice beads of sweat on his forehead, the way his tongue sweeps across his bottom lip like he wants a taste not unnoticed.

"I want everyone to write three paragraphs on... um," he scrambles as he quickly steps behind his desk to mask his hard-on. "Write about your thoughts on author Harper Lee," he mumbles nervously. Everyone opens their laptop, lost in their task, but I continue to watch the professor.

When will we get alone time again?

He looks at me as he jerks open the bottom drawer to his desk and pulls out a bottle of lotion. He shakes his head at me with a playful smile and my mouth drops. I want to be the one sliding my lotioned hands up and down his shaft, not him. I caused that excitement, I want to play with it. Turning his back to me, he enters his private bathroom to the right of his desk.

I lose it, I double over and laugh so hard it echoes in the auditorium.

Professor Prescott leaves his bathroom fifteen minutes later, the lotion bottle left behind. He looks down at himself, his hands smoothing out his slacks as he shuts the door behind him. He glances up at the clock and notices the session is over.

"I'll see you guys tomorrow." He clears his throat, his eyes peeking at me before he heads to his desk. Putting my stuff in my bag, I head to him. He bundles up folders and books as if he's leaving and I frown.

"I have a meeting, but I'll catch you later?" He hands me a note, and I take it.

"Okay," I mutter disappointed.

Just as he steps past me he stops, his lips near my ear and his breath hot.

"See what you do to me?"

I bite my bottom lip to keep from smiling. When he leaves I

open the folded note. I feel like a schoolgirl opening a note from a crush, it's exhilarating.

Meet me in the library at five.

———

STANDING IN THE LIBRARY, my fingers run along the books placed perfectly on the shelves. The smell of old paper and ink is relaxing. It's five o'clock on the dot, and I'm a mess of nerves. I picked a secluded spot for me and the professor and wore my cutest dress and best perfume. This evening, things are going to happen. I can feel it in my chest that we are going to bond, get closer than ever.

Something catches my eye from outside the window next to me and I turn toward it. Thunder echoes in the old building as I watch Professor Prescott heading toward the library. My cheeks warm and my heart pounds a little faster at the sight of him. He's coming to see me.

He stops and looks behind him and that's when I see June in the parking lot. She says something to him, and he points to the library.

"Tell her you have plans," I will him. My breath fogging the window. My fingernails biting into my palms with anticipation. She shakes her head and waves him over. He hesitantly turns and heads toward her, and my stomach falls. What is he doing?

He pulls June in close to his chest, the passion evident between their body language. She has a bundle of books held above their heads trying to ward off the rain and he tries to kiss her, and she laughs, pulling away from him with a sultry look on her face. It's the notorious rain scene in every romance novel.

My hand clasps around my throat as I feel I might be sick at any moment.

I watch from the window as they both climb into their Range Rover and leave together. Professor Michael Prescott leaves me behind.

My breathing begins to pick up, my heart feeling like a puppet that's had its strings torn from its limbs and thrown to the side in a sick game.

Pulling my gaze from the window I take a step in the direction of the library doors only to run smack into someone.

"MOVE IT!" I glower, not paying attention to who is in my way.

Once my feet hit the outside pavement, rain pours off the roof, soaking me. Water sticks to my lashes as I watch the professor and his wife drive away from the school.

He said he didn't want to be with her. So why did he choose her over me?

"He lied," I grit. "He fucking lied!" A young man wearing a yellow rain jacket looks at me crazily as he darts inside the library.

Turning in the rain, I bite my bottom lip, the sharp teeth piercing the flesh painfully.

He led me on, toyed with my emotions like a puppet on a string. He loves her, you could see it on his face when he was holding her. He cares for her.

I want to get angry, but if I do, Harley will come forward and I won't get any answers.

Instead, I begin to tear up, my heart crashing in my chest. I feel dirty. Unwanted, and ashamed. I blow out a sad breath, my fingers flexing in and out in an attempt to control my temper.

The butterflies in my stomach that were from the professor go up in flames and a heartfelt scream erupts from my mouth as I let the pain out.

———

STANDING outside a two-story house with perfect rose bushes placed along the front lawn, a stone walkway lights up from the most expensive lights I've ever seen. I watch as Professor

Prescott parks his black shiny car inside the left side of the garage.

Thunder cracks from above and rain pelts into my thin summer dress. It's cold, the droplets feeling like ice daggers. My nostrils flare watching him, my heart pounding as it cracks and bleeds at my feet.

My chest feels tight like I can't breathe. This heartbroken feeling is not worth the trouble I went through with this man. I wasted my freedom on him when I could have been with someone else that actually cared about me. Look at this house. It's family material with its perfect lawn, and perfect street, and perfect neighborhood.

I was played. The common teacher-student romance just became my reality.

Forcing myself to move, I head toward the big house.

Smoothing my wet, wrinkly dress out, I knock on the door and muster a smile.

"You know I hate it when you park there, I have to squeeze behind your car to get to the door!" a female voice screams in dismay.

"It's always about you June, isn't it!" Professor Prescott hollers back. "Why don't you just call your fucking daddy and tell him to have his men build us a bigger garage, or better yet—"

I knock again, but louder this time. The hollering hushes, and clicking against the floor becomes louder just before the door is jerked opened.

"Farrah?" June remembers me.

"Hi June, I'm here for my tutoring session," I lie, but I need to see the professor. Her brows furrow before she looks over her shoulder at her husband. She smells... expensive. Seeing her in her own house I see how much money she is made of. How materialistic she really is.

He clears his throat, his eyes ablaze when they land on me.

"Uh, yeah. I just forgot," he shrugs, rubbing the back of his neck anxiously. He's not good at lying. Which I like, he's different than the club. The whole reason I thought he was different.

June forces a smile, her eyes raking me up and down like I intimidate her. My hair hangs heavily, drenched and clumping together, and my dress feels like it's ten times heavier, so the notion is ridiculous right now.

"Come in, let me get you a towel," she says with a bored tone before walking away.

She left the door opened before stepping away, so I take it upon myself to enter. It smells like a brand-new house. No dirt on the floor, no clothes flung around. In fact, it doesn't even look like a couple lives here. For a house so clean, the closet sure is filled with skeletons.

"You have a really nice house," I admire, looking around. It's expensive, I wonder if the governor bought it.

A hand grabs around my shoulder yanking me backward.

It's him. Michael, I'd know the touch from anywhere. It's soft and simple. The smell of pencil shavings and chalk takes over my senses. I used to find it sexy, now it reminds me of a kindergartner.

"What the fuck are you doing here?" he whispers harshly in my ear.

I smile.

"Aren't you happy to see me?" I wink, grabbing at his pant buttons recklessly. Showing up unannounced was a risk, but one I wanted and needed to take. If June finds out about us, then it's for the best. He's about to find out I'm one girl he can't walk on.

"Are you insane?" he quips. That stings, but I push it back. He didn't mean it.

"Shh, you can fuck me while the wife watches if you want," I suggest, and I notice his Adam's apple bob from my suggestion. I'm way out of line, and I find it exciting.

"There's something wrong with you," he struggles with his words, almost like a cry for help.

"You forgot me." I narrow my eyes at him, my reckless behavior fading into how I'm really feeling.

"You... You can't be here. Do you realize what you're doing being here? Her father is going to kill me!" He slaps at my hands, and I'd think he was joking about her father killing him if fear wasn't so evident in his face.

I rub my palm along his face.

"Poor, poor, teacher," I coo, and his head whips up, insulted.

"Michael has never tutored any of his students before." June's voice sounds just around the corner and Professor Prescott pulls away from me, causing me to sway on my feet.

June stops when she enters the foyer, her eyes driving into me like a pair of pear knifes.

"I guess I'm just special." I give her a pointed look, and she crosses her arms. She's not jealous, she looks embarrassed more than anything. What? A little schoolgirl appearing at your door for help with her homework hurt her image of governor's daughter?

I step up to her and grab the fluffy yellow towel. My fingers never felt something so soft before, I can't help but bring it to my face and inhale its fresh laundry scent. I wonder if she washes them herself, or if she has a maid?

"Thanks!" I whisper, never taking my eyes off hers.

The room fills with tension, June staring at Michael, Michael staring at me.

I turn and look around. A picture of June, Michael, and an older man, grabbing my attention sitting on the counter. It's the only thing on the counter actually. As if they want to prove their relationship to everyone who enters their empty home.

I grab it for a closer look.

"This is lovely." I rub my pruned finger along the glass.

"That is my father. Timothy the governor," June explains behind me.

The older man has a tight grip on Michael, but the way he

looks at him, I can tell he depends on Michael more than his own daughter. I bite my inner cheek in thought. Michael appears to be scared of Timothy, and from what I understand Timothy is a dangerous man if he's in with the club. I look over my shoulder at Michael, curious if he's just as dangerous as the governor or if he's just another prick in the palm of the governor's hand.

"Are you and your father close, June?" I can't help but ask as I set the picture down.

"Can I get you a glass of water or something?" June asks, ignoring my question.

A chill runs up my arm and I rub the towel along my cooled skin.

The sentence echoes in my head and my chest tightens. A little girl in a trailer is soaking wet, a hurt expression on her face. My chest burns as I realize it's Harley. An image that burns in the back of my mind every time someone asks me for a fucking glass of anything.

My stomach clenches and anger drums in the temples of my head. This is too much. All of it. Him choosing her, seeing them in their home. I shouldn't be here.

"I have to go," I reply quickly, dropping the towel.

"What about your session?" June asks, reaching out to me.

"I just remembered I have something to do." I toss over my shoulder, not having time to come up with a better lie.

"Let me drive you, it's pouring," Professor Prescott insists, coming after me.

He grabs my shoulder stopping me. God his touch is divine. I hate to love it.

"This way." He forces my body in the direction of the garage.

"I can walk, really," I shrug, needing to be far away from him. It's not safe. I need out of here and now. I'm upset with him and need space.

"*KILL HIM! Show your club what you're made of!*" Rings in my head so hard it sounds like a siren. A whirl of emotions slamming against each other, fighting over the spotlight.

I hunch over, my fingers tangling in my hair. I don't want to be pushed to the side. I need to be here. I have so much left to do.

"Farrah? Are you okay?" His hand slides up my back in a suggestive manner, his wife just inside. His touch makes me want to vomit. My chest rattles with anger and sadness. I feel so stupid thinking he'd choose me.

"Are you sick?" he mutters. That one sentence makes me cringe every time I hear it. I could answer it with an act of murder, a smile on my face and blood on my hands. I'm the fucking poster child for mental illness, put upon my head a bloody tiara and I would wear it proudly, or should I say... Harley would wear it with devil grin.

"You just – you just left me behind without a second glance," I manage to choke out. His touch stills on my back and the room goes quiet. I stand upright and look him in the eye. "Am I so lucky to be the only girl you play with on the side or are there others?" I tilt my head to the side, tears streaming down my face.

"What did you expect, Farrah?" He laughs, placing his hands on his hips. I close my eyes, the feeling of my chest being pulled apart so painful I can't be here a second longer.

He's a douchebag, and I'm stupid for believing we were each other's happiness.

Hands curled into my chest, I run out of the garage and shoot off into the rain. My legs having their own mind I sprint toward campus and don't look back. It's better this way because if I stay my hurt will turn to anger, and Harley will come to the light.

I don't know what her mission is with the professor but with her, I'm sure it's something grim and I'm not done talking to the professor about how to treat girls and their hearts.

By the time I reach my dorm my skin is clear of any makeup, tattoos on my arms showing fully as the concealer I placed on them has washed away. I'm slowly becoming Harley.

I can feel anger, rage, and darkness filling my head. Harley. Everything that keeps her company in the shadows is snuffing out the light inside of me.

Staggering up the stairs, I make my way to the second floor. My head aches and my legs shake. I fall against the wall, tearing down missing posters, and sign-up sheets for Drama Club.

"You okay?" A cheerleader looking chick asks.

"Fuck off or I'll slit your throat!" I swipe at her, and she screams and runs. I cover my mouth, the words surprising me. I'd never say that to anyone.

Heaving, stumbling, I make it to my room and shut the door. My knees crumble, and I face plant to the floor.

12

HARLEY

My eyes flutter open, the side of my face burning as if I just dragged it along the carpeted floor. My cheek hurts, and I raise my hand to inspect it.

"Ouch." I wince. I must have taken a hard fall. It's not the worst of my falls, though. I came to once on the stairs at the club and had to get stitches at the base of my head.

Groaning, I pull myself up off the floor and look around the room.

I'm in the dorm room I rented out when I came to campus. Why am I cold and damp? Looking down I find myself wearing a stupid fucking dress. Farrah...

Oh no, Farrah was in the light.

"No," I whisper to myself. My fingers rubbing along the material of the dress. I try to remember the last thing I did, but it's all black. I can't remember anything before getting set up in my room. Biting my lip, I notice my lip ring missing. Cursing under my breath, I stagger to the mirror on the wall, curious what else Farrah did to my appearance.

I gasp in horror, clutching my mouth.

My hair, it's colored brown and pink. My blonde hair, it's gone. My piercings are gone too. I look... different.

"Noooo!" I scream angrily, clearing everything off the sink in a fit of fury. Pretty makeup and girly shit go flying across the room. "YOU FUCKING BITCH, FARRAH!" I shout to no one but myself. Farrah can't hear me, so my yelling at her is pointless.

"I'm trying to study!" muffled yelling from the room next to mine, a fist pounding on the wall to follow.

"Shut the fuck up," I scream at the girl next door. Grabbing a blow dryer off the sink I throw it at the wall, and the pounding stops.

"You fuck everything up, you ruin everything," I cry softly as I fall to the floor on my hands and knees. Adrenaline pulses through me so hard I feel high. I'm so angry and so hurt. This was my only chance at finding myself, and my illness had to show its ugly head and fuck everything up.

Standing on wobbly legs, I clutch the cold sink and close my eyes. I try to breathe, try to calm myself, but it's no use. She went too far this time. Farrah, went too far this time.

A laptop suddenly illuminates from my bed, the professor's picture expanded. *Where did that laptop come from? How could Farrah afford it?* I slide my finger along the pad bringing up the bottom toolbar. September 1st. My head falls with despair. Days of my life are gone. Drifted in the black abyss that I'll never get back. I got here four fucking days ago. Farrah came to the light right after check-in and has been running around the campus living my life.

"Fuck, fuck, fuck," I whisper under my breath. Hot tears stream down my cheeks as I close my eyes. I try to bring forward some memory to indicate if Farrah has interacted with the professor, but I can't remember a thing. I never can. It's like a wall, a thick brick wall I can't climb over, under, or through. I'm left in the darkness where the other side holds the light.

Wiping the tears from my face, I grab the computer and face it toward me.

Clicking the laptop's history, there's nothing but information on the professor. She's been stalking him.

"Goddamn it," I growl. She *has* been in contact with him. My heart strikes in my chest with my next thought. I pray she didn't sleep with him. I've only slept with Benji, and the memory of our first time is one I think about every night before going to bed. Farrah sleeping with someone else makes me feel... violated. She's a slut and wants someone to love her so badly... she'll destroy me if it means she gets her happily ever after.

She ruins everything.

My fingers still on the keyboard the skull ring that was Benji's shines on my thumb. *Where is he? Maybe I should call him. With Farrah coming out, everything has changed.*

I climb over to my leather bag tucked away in the corner and dump the contents. The orange pill bottles I'm looking for don't fall out of the bag. Gasping for air, I shove my hand in the bag hoping they got stuck or something, but it's empty. I forgot them.

Without me taking them for days, Farrah will be back.

My therapist says Farrah and I should work together, but that will never happen. I take the meds, she doesn't. She wants to live her own life, and I want my own.

One time I came to in the middle of a storm stranded on a beach in Texas. I had no recollection of how I got there, all I had on was a stupid sundress surrounded by a bunch of spring breakers thinking it was cool to party in the midst of a hurricane. I had no personal items on me and had to borrow a cell phone from some drunk chick by a campfire to get ahold of Benji.

He took care of everything and got me back home safely. But still, it makes me wonder with every living second, whenever I blink or simply just breathe... Where will I be next? What will I do? What would it be that led me there?

Falling to my ass, my knees to my chest, my eyes fall on a

picture of me and Benji that fell from my bag. It's one of my favorites.

It's from one of the club parties. I'm wearing his leather cut because I was cold, my cut-off shorts showing my tan tattooed legs. I have a beer in my hand and a smile on my face as Benji surprisingly pulled me into a hug from behind. He's my best friend and I miss him so much.

Sobbing, I grab it and clutch it to my chest.

I miss him, more than I thought I ever would, right now.

He'd know what to do if he were here. He knows how to handle Farrah, make her sink within.

Leaning my head against the wall, I shake my head. Coming here was stupid, I knew there was a possibility Farrah would come forth.

Sliding to the floor, I lay my head on the carpet and close my eyes. I try to breathe through my pain, my anger, and torment. How I long to be normal, to be just... me.

"*Stay still,*" echoes through my head and a small smile slips past my agony.

The few words that Benji would whisper to me after an episode.

"*Why do you keep saying that?*" *I ask, clawing at him as if I could climb inside of him and wear him as protection. A cloak of some kind to protect myself from myself.* "*Like staying still will make everything better!*" *I sob.*

"*Can you feel my heart beat against your back?*" *he asks softly. I nod, I can feel it. It's pounding hard, and steady.* "*Can you hear only my voice?*" *I look up at him, his chin to my forehead. His voice rough with a growl, but soft like silk the way it wrapped around me and grounded me. Kept me safe.*

"*The chaos and the voices can't be heard if you stay still and let me have you,*" *he insists. The stubble of his chin scratching along my forehead.*

"Stay still," I whisper, trying to pretend that Benji is here with me now. His voice, his hard heartbeat against my back. His arms wrapped around me, protecting me. "Stay still..."

Benji

Reaching the campus, I park right in front of the main building. I am not fucking with a parking garage and stupid ass college kids dinging my doors with their beat-up shit. The smell of rain hangs in the air, and kids amongst all ages walk around oblivious to who the fuck just showed up on their front doorstep and who they've been living amongst for days. The fucking Shadow Keepers Enforcer, and their princess.

Sliding my hands through my dark hair, I pull my cut tighter around my shoulders and start toward the main office.

Girls flash me a flirtatious smile, and boys look at me as if I'm lost. It's the leather cut, the large rings on my fingers, and the bold tattoos on my skin that grabs everyone's respect.

I sneer. Fucking college. Out of all the places I've gone to get Harley, this has to be the worst.

Hipsters and spoiled ass brats get on my nerves more than anything.

13

FARRAH

Waking up this morning, I pick out a cute pink frilly dress and pull off the black panties and bra Harley put on last night. Her idea of a wardrobe is so trashy, you could compare it to a homeless person. Smoothing out my dress, I pluck the lip ring out of my lip and reach for the concealer on the counter. I smother the tattoos on my arms, the color so vibrant it needs an extra coat. Harley really should have consulted with me before she did this to my body.

Grabbing my school bag, I flip my dark hair over my shoulder and head toward class. I can't wait to see Professor Prescott. I'm not done with him yet. I demand answers and I will get them. I just have to remain calm about it. I bite my lip, curious if Harley has gotten to see him yet. I hope not because he might be alive if she has.

Stepping outside the dorm's building, a chill crawls through the trees, and I stop on the bottom step of the building. Slowly I look over my shoulder, feeling drawn to something powerful. It's as if the whole campus is under a spell, moving slower and cautious today.

My eyes fall on Benjamin, and I suck in a ragged breath. He's dark and handsome and sticks out in the crowd of young kids. "Fuck," I mumble under my breath. He's here for Harley. Turning around quickly before we make eye contact I make my way to the auditorium. I remain stiff and keep my head down. If he sees me, he'll throw me over his shoulder and march me out of this campus not giving a fuck who sees. Just as I reach my class, I hurry inside and find my seat just as professor scribbles our daily assignment on the board. Slumping in my seat, I release a full breath. I watch the professor in fascination, remembering our time together at that very desk. The way he looked at me, his muscles tensing with restraint. The way my hair felt wrapped around his hand, the roughness of his touch as he forced me to bend forward.

My eyes flutter with sudden sadness. I thought it was him acting on the pull between us, not him preying on young girls.

"I want you all to write a short story on something controversial and where you stand on the topic," he informs. Flicking my pencil against my desk, I watch him closely as he walks back and forth across the room. The way his shiny shoes tap against the floor with each step, the bulge in his slacks when they stretch. He's not looking at me though, not even a glance. My heart sags in my chest, my nostrils flaring. We usually play a sexual staring game in every class, one that has me blushing and looking down. He smirks, and continues his lecture. But not today...

Our game is over.

I stare at him the entire time class is in session, willing him to look my way. I'm not sure what I'll do if he does look this way. Flip him off, pout, or let Harley take over. I just want him to acknowledge me.

He smiles, his eyes directed toward the top of the auditorium. Frowning I follow his eyesight and see a new girl in paint covered overalls and pigtails sitting at the top. She is nibbling on a blue pencil, one of the professor's. She winks at him, and I quickly turn around. My fingernails impaling the top of my desk.

THAT BASTARD.

"Class dismissed," he clips before sitting behind his desk. I shake my head, coming to the fact class is over and he's cold-shouldered me the whole time. He's moved on to his next toy and forgotten me.

I wait for everyone to leave, the girl in the overalls waits too, but I'm not going anywhere so she can take a hike. I make my way to him. Needing to talk to him and now. I glare at the girl in pigtails, my eyes digging into her like sharp table knives. Getting the hint, she quickly packs her books and scurries away.

Satisfied that it's just me and the professor, I exhale a breath loud enough to draw his attention.

"Something I can help you with?" he asks in a formal tone that manages to cut me straight to the bone. He acts as if we haven't been playing this cat and mouse game from the very beginning.

"Why are you ignoring me?" I ask with emotion in my voice.

He looks up at me, his eyes cold.

"This is over. I can't have you showing up at my house and risking my life," he confesses and my eyes bug out. *His life?* Is he serious?

"Are you happy?" I can't help but ask. Knowing he's not, in fact, I bet his father-in-law has something over him. Does Harley know this? Is this why she's after him?

He shakes his head in an irritated manner.

"It doesn't matter. All you need to know is this is over." He looks down, red pen in his hand.

"You think this is okay?" I scoff, and he sighs, avoiding looking at me. He can't get rid of me that easily.

I step around the desk to him, and he sighs leaning back in his chair. Taking the opportunity, I climb on his lap, my legs straddling his. The smell of pencil shavings and permanent marker strong. Grabbing his tie, I pull his face inches within mine.

"Tell me you don't want me," I whisper with anger in my voice. I need to hear him say it. The final vessel in my heart to be slit and bleed out.

He opens his mouth to talk, but shuts it quickly.

I situate myself on the bulge in his pants, and a tingle shoots through my limbs. I close my eyes, hating I still want him after knowing we have nothing but a sexual pull.

"Tell me to stop," I breathe heavily. Please for the love of God tell me to stop.

His hands grasp my bare thighs and my head falls back with satisfaction. He slides his palms upward, his knuckles brushing my dress to the side as it hikes further up.

"Why am I attracted to the crazy bitches?" he moans, and my wet panties stick to my pussy as I rock myself back and forth on him.

A bang echoes through the room, and he shoves me off of him as he jumps from his seat. We both look around the room, looking for any form of disturbance, but there's nobody. Pigtail girl is long gone.

"Look, I can't do this. I'm having you removed from class, and I don't want to see you again, Farrah." He looks up at me with hooded eyes. There it is, the nail in the coffin. His coffin.

My nostrils flare, hot tears filling my vision.

His hands on the desk, his back arched as he bends over to catch his breath, he shakes his head.

"This... this is over," He breathes heavily.

I can feel the rage building in my chest, my heart throbbing in my throat. I try to ease my emotions, knowing if I don't, Harley will take the front seat, and this will all be over before it started.

He reaches for a glass of water on his desk, and the sight of it makes my head throb. The glass looks familiar with the flower sketching on the side.

Closing my eyes, I see a little girl in the trailer, soaked. Her mother holding a glass just like the one the professor has. It's Harley, and she's upset, scared even.

Screaming out of control, I grab his desk and flip it over, my strength surprising me. My face red and veins protruding from my neck. I lower my head and glare at him with a darkness that dwells within that can only be Harley.

"You're going to pay for breaking my heart," I seethe.

14

HARLEY

Glass crashes to the floor and Professor Prescott stands there looking at me with wide eyes and the biggest bulge I've seen in a pair of dress slacks.

I look around me. I'm in some sort of classroom or something.

"Farrah?" Prescott asks timidly; scared even. I turn, my cheeks warm, and my panties wet and sticking to me uncomfortably. I hate panties. There's tension in the air and the desk is flipped over with debris everywhere. Something bad just happened.

"What'd you do?" I ask, my chest rising and falling rapidly. He must have hurt Farrah, why else would I be here. She wouldn't let me come to the front so easily, she wants me here. My hands slide along soft material, and I notice I'm in a damn dress again.

"Me?" he scoffs, but I'm done asking questions.

My eyes fall to the broken glass on the floor, water pooling around it. Bending down, I grasp the glass, my palm cutting into the sharp edge and staining the water on the floor beneath my feet. Standing with the shard of glass in my hand, I point it at him.

He holds his hands up. "What the fuck did you do?" I seethe, demanding an answer now.

"Whoa!" His face pales as if he's looking at me for the very first time. The real me.

Harley Vander.

Students crowd into the auditorium and I grit my teeth. It's time for the next class. I'll have to wait to kill him, I guess.

"You'll regret this," I hiss, dropping the shard of glass. My palm stings from the cut, but I don't let on. There's a far more painful tinge in my chest, and I'm guessing the professor is the cause for it.

I may not care for Farrah as she fucks everything up, but nobody fucks with her.

Stomping out of the auditorium the wind shifts, reeling in a new air. One that is colder, hostile, and willing the true colors of who I am. I'm going to fuck this campus up.

I need to do what I came for and get the fuck out of here.

Head down, I head to my room. I'm going to get the professor and the fucking governor to pay up what he owes my club. I just have to figure out how. Opening the door to my room, I slam it shut. Hysteria climbing up my throat until a violent roar fills the room.

He was right there, I could have easily kidnapped that wimpy suggestion of a man but fucking witnesses had to ruin it.

"Harley?" My head slowly turns finding Benji standing in the corner of the room with his arms crossed.

Taking a step forward he musses his hair with his hand, his blue Caribbean eyes staring at me. He's wearing a sleeveless shirt under his club cut. The sight of worn leather bringing me home.

"Benji!" I cry, running into his arms.

His large arms wrap around me and I close my eyes. The smell of leather, weed, and spice makes me inhale a large breath and hold it in. God, he feels so good. I missed him.

"What is wrong?" He senses my unease. His lips press into the top of my head. His hand slowly rubbing up and down my back in a comforting manner.

"He... did something to Farrah," I whisper into his hard chest. Benji warned me since we were kids not to trust any man. That having a split personality disorder, only he could tell who I really was, and who my alters were.

Benji freezes in my hold.

"Who?"

"The professor."

I pull away, wiping the lone tear off from my face.

"The professor? Did you sleep with him?" he seethes, his tone turning from caring to dominant. "DID YOU?" he roars, jealousy ringing in my ears. I turn, looking at him. Seeing him so jealous is a turn on but it breaks my heart at the same time. As much as I want Benji, I wish he'd leave us at being friends as I will only hurt him in the end. Can't he see that.

"Answer me!" He steps forward, his figure taking up the entire dorm room.

"I don't know!" I hate my life. How I live from one blackout to the next. "My blackouts are worse, Farrah has taken over—"

"It's worse because you forgot your fucking medication at the club, Harley," Benji schools, his tone of voice rougher than he's ever spoken to me before. I glare over my shoulder, shaking my head.

Launching forward he grabs me by the hips and throws me over his knee.

"What are you doing?" I toss my hair from my face, my legs and arms sprawled out awkwardly. Benji raises his arm and strikes my ass cheek. My hard nipples press into his legs, my body tingling with unexpected desire. One, two, three, four times he spanks me like a child before standing me upright.

I stand there confused, hair in my face and my butt cheek stinging. I pull the dress up, revealing red handprints staining my butt. It's so fucking hot to see. The dominant, controlling side of Benji is undoing my restraint.

"You had me fucking worried sick, Harley!" He gets in my

face, but I'm still trying to piece together what just happened, and why I liked it so much. He spanked me, he fucking spanked me. I didn't feel like a child though, I felt naughty.

"Why are you here?" I tilt my head to the side, trying to change the subject. I need all things spanking out of my head, and now. I mean, I knew he'd find me, I just didn't realize how quickly. He's crazy if he thinks I'm just going to leave.

Stomping forward, he grabs me by the neck with a firm grip. It's dominant, and the graze of his thumb against the hollow of my neck doesn't go unnoticed. His touch callused but passionate. I swallow, looking into the eyes of who Benji really is. The Enforcer of the Shadow Keepers MC, not the little boy I grew up with.

Maybe that's where I've gone wrong this whole time.

I saw Benji as the boy downstairs who snuck weed from our fathers for us to smoke in the motorcycle graveyard, rather than the Enforcer of the Shadow Keepers MC. A killer, drug dealer, and outlaw the police can never catch. He's much too smart and strong for that.

"I'm here because I fucking care! Because no matter how many times you try to friend zone me, I am *your* man. I fucked that pussy first, and I will be the only one to ever be in between those legs. You better fucking realize that, and quick. Because I'm tired of worshipping a crazy bitch that doesn't even know it!"

Worship? The word makes me suck in a tight breath.

"How? How can you want to be with me when you don't even know who I really am?" I cry, shoving him away with frustration. Having a split personality disorder steals your life, and you live from blackout to blackout. It's no way to live, and having a relationship is out of the question.

His brows pinch forward with rage.

"Because I don't give a fuck who you think you are or how fucked up you might really be. I love your crazy ass, and I would do anything for you. You're just too stupid to see that!" He points to his head in anger, his tone rough and furious. "Don't you see. Farrah, Harley, who the fuck you might be... it's all you. They are all pieces of you split up to help you cope with shit you can't do by yourself."

A tear slides down my cheek, my backside now on fire from where he hit me.

"You make it sound so simple," I mutter. Why can't I just do drugs or become depressed to deal with stress. Why do I have to have these demons taking over my life?

"It is. You just need to figure out when this all started and figure out why Farrah was created to help you cope." His hands stretched out wide as if the bigger picture lies within his palms.

"What? Did you talk to a doctor or something?" I scoff. I've looked my condition up, I know everything he's saying, but to hear that he set club business to the side to try and help me become better. It does something to me. It makes me feel normal. Wanted. Loved.

I've blacked out and woken up confused all my life. Personalities have come and gone, but Farrah, she's always here.

"Can I have a glass of water, Mommy?" echoes in my head like a bad tune.

I close my eyes. Urging the words out of my head. I don't even know what they mean. I just know when I hear them... everything goes black. My teeth clash as if they might break. I feel... different.

It's said that there is no cure for what I have, but sometimes if you can figure out why the alters were created, such as abuse or some kind of trauma, and cope with it. The alter that was created to deal with whatever happened, will disappear.

I just don't know why Farrah was created in the first place. If I did, maybe then we could cope together.

"It doesn't matter!" I reply in frustration, wiping the tears from my face.

I turn, looking him in the eyes. The stupid dress skirting

around my legs making me feel vulnerable, I cross my arms and look around the room for my leather jacket.

"I needed to prove I belong to the Shadow Keepers. That I can handle a job," I explain.

He cups my throat, lowering his head in a menacing way.

"You belong in that club more than any of us, but we're a brotherhood, we do shit together. You running off by yourself putting yourself at risk proves you are not ready to sit at the table regardless if you have dick, pussy, or fucked up in the head," he scorns, and my eyes widen to saucers with revelation. He's right, the club is a team. No one manhandles shit on their own. That's why they're a brotherhood. They work together with common end goals.

His lips graze along the shell of my ear, and instead of pushing him away like I normally do, I sink into him for more. I've never been so scared in my life, and having Benji here I feel safe. It shows me how much I really care about him and need him. I'm ready to take on why I came here in the first place.

"God, I missed you," he whispers, "both of you." His broad nose rubs amongst the soft skin of my neck as he breathes me in and unwinds the hostility wrapping around us.

My head lolls back, his hands on my hips. My sex pulses with need, wanting so badly to have Benji explore my body. I've never forgotten my first time with Benji, it was perfect. He's been the only guy I've been with.

His left hand snakes up my dress and grasps my right tit firmly. My nipple buds and aches for more.

"This is insane. Us together is crazy," I pant, my head and heart battling with what is right and wrong.

I want Benji, I do. But my condition is not fair to him, I'd be selfish allowing us to turn into something.

I push him away and turn around panting for air.

"What the fuck, Harley!" he growls, angry with my teasing.

I shake my head and look at the floor. It's not my intention to lead him on. I want him, I do so fucking bad, but every time I let myself think for a second I am capable of loving him. My father's words come to mind.

"Stay away from that boy. You're not right, Harley. You can't love anyone because your heart isn't whole. It's split up, and it's unfair to love with only half of your heart."

"I can't love someone, Benji," I explain.

"I've loved you since we were fucking kids," he says calmly. I peer at him behind my bangs. He said he loved me. He's never said that to me. It breaks down barriers I can't keep up if I tried. Lifting his cut, he pulls out a worn blue notebook and unexpectedly tosses it at me.

I catch it before it hits the ground, my brows furrowing at what it might be.

"I'm starting to think you just keep me around so you're not alone," he rasps, his statement a slap in the face. I am alone because nobody wants to be friends with an insane person.

"That's not true," I frown. How can he think that? I care about Benji, that's why I am pushing him away not because I'm scared of being alone.

"Well, I'm done being your fucking puppet, Harley."

I open my mouth to speak, but the words of hurt slip off my tongue as the smoothness of the worn notebook caresses my fingertips. The door slams behind him, and I hang my head. I may have just lost my best friend.

I open the pages of the blue notebook. My eyes filling with tears as I look at the pages. My mouth parts in astonishment. My hand presses against my lips as my heart is torn apart and put back together in a matter of seconds.

"Oh my God," I whisper. My tongue slipping across my bottom lip, the taste of my tears filling my mouth.

Dating back to when we were kids there are names, and descriptions of every alter I've ever had.

Mia – Nine Years Old-

Mia likes art but doesn't like me. Her mother is a painter and her father died on the job as a firefighter. She always has ink or paint on her clothes, and dresses like a hippie.

Farrah – Nine Years Old-

Farrah wears dresses and heels from the club girls. She flirts with me, and every boy she comes across. Her feelings are hurt easily though, so I have to be careful. When she's upset she's dangerous.

Billy – Ten Years Old-

Billy is rough and likes to wrestle. He thinks the club is cool but instead of jackets, we should wear capes.

A small laugh racks my body reading the cape part, and I turn a few pages.

Aria – Fifteen-

Very religious, scared of the club and always hides in the club's freezer. She hates the color black and makes me pray with her often. She's odd.

Farrah – Fifteen

Farrah tried to sleep with one of the hang arounds today, and I ended up hitting him in the head with a wrench from the garage. Dad was pissed. Farrah comes and goes, but one thing is persistent. She wants love, just not with me.

Hastily, I turn three more pages.

Peyton – Seventeen-

Angry with the world, tired of not being around kids her age and is self-destructive. She cut herself on purpose in her bathroom upstairs. I cleaned it up and even stitched her arm the best I could from a YouTube video we found so Harley's dad would never know.

My eyes fall to the tattoo on my forearm, the tree line of ink covering the scar. I remember coming to with stitches there when I was seventeen. Benji told me everything was going to be all right but not what had happened. I was tired of being lost and confused. Anxiety so high I was losing my shit. He cocooned me until we fell to the roof of the club. He whispered in my ear, *"Learn to get lost a little bit, baby."* The words struck every chord in my heart. Learn to get lost. As if I should embrace the blackouts, and enjoy the journey of the unknown. In life we're supposed to have our shit together, be prepared, and organized. But when life takes a turn into the unknown, we panic.

What if we learn to embrace that panic? We stop and watch those who are on autopilot drive by while we take a moment and get lost. Get away from life, and all the bull shit.

WHEN THE WOUND was healed Benji paid for my first tattoo to cover up the scar. My fingers rub along the saying underneath the intricate forest etched into my skin.

"Learn to get lost a little bit." I didn't put 'baby' because I didn't want Benji to think anything more than us as friends, but when I look at the words, the small space after 'bit,' I see the word baby. I hear it in my head as if it was just yesterday. I feel it in my heart, right down to the very vessel that makes it beat.

I slam the notebook shut, the lump in my throat hard to swallow. Benji has been loving me every day we've been in each other's life. Every little piece of me since we were kids. If he can love the crazy in me, why can't I love him back with the pieces I have to offer?

I may not be perfect for him, but I am good enough for him.

I need to find Benji.

15

HARLEY

S hoving my leather boots on and clutching the notebook
to my chest I run down the stairs and outside into
the night.

"Benji!" I scream, needing to find him before he leaves or does
something I'll never forgive him for. Like screwing another girl,
and me walking in on it.

Looking around I hear laughter behind the next building and
head toward the only noise on campus. Rounding the building I
find Benji leaning against his sexy car, his feet crossed in front of
him and a joint hanging out of his mouth. There are four girls
hanging around him and his car. Jealousy burns in my chest like
a forest fire; out of control.

I step to them slowly, trying to keep my temper reeled in.

Benji's blue eyes land on mine and butterflies fill my stomach.
I want him, I want him so fucking bad I'd fuck him on the hood
of his car in front of everyone just to prove how much I've loved
him over the years. I'm not holding back a second longer
anymore.

That notebook, it changed everything.

A blonde who has been in the tanning bed way too much sees Benji staring at me with hooded eyes and stands straight.

Placing her hands on her hips she glares at me like I'm interrupting something.

"Hey, Private Ryan called, he wants his boots back," she insults, and the other girls laugh. Benji just exhales a cloud of smoke as he watches.

I look to the sky, asking the Lord to give me strength not to kill this bitch tonight.

I lift the notebook and look to Benji. "Is this true. Have you been journaling every alter?" I ask with a trembling voice.

He gives a curt nod, and I choke on my next words. It's too much. I've never had anyone do something so personal before.

"Aw, are you going to cry?" the tanned blonde taunts, knowing nothing of what me and Benji are talking about. Needing an outlet for the emotions running through me, my hand clenches to form a fist as I raise it and crack her in the nose with my fist.

Adrenaline rushes down my arm and spreads through my hand in the form of pain.

She screams bloody murder, blood pouring from her face as I shake my hand out. Her friends run to her, and Benji takes another hit from his joint as if nothing is happening. Striding up next to him, I grab the joint from his lips and take a rip. The smoke rolls in my mouth and I blow it into his face.

Our eyes never leaving one another as the chaos behind us erupts.

"She has a photoshoot tomorrow for the cheerleading calendar!" one of the girls yells out as they help their stupid friend to the dorms. Both Benji and I lost in our own little world, we ignore them. Come to think of it, we've always been in our own little world.

Earth spins, the sun rises and sets, but Benji and I have always been side by side, our eyes locked on each other.

"I... I was wrong," I admit, and his lips quirk at the corner. He's loving this.

"Harley Vander, wrong..." he mutters looking out into the campus.

"Don't rub it in, asshole." I nudge him with my elbow. "How? How did all those alters leave, but Farrah stuck around?" I shrug.

Benji sighs, his stance widening.

"Maybe the reason they came to the front was reconciled?" he asks more than answers. Benji has always been there to save me, but this condition I have... is one time Benji can't rescue me.

He grips me behind the neck, the touch hardening as he turns me around and shoves me up against his car with haste. My fingers release the joint, my mouth parting with desire. His controlling touch ignites a pulsing need deep inside of me.

"You're *MY* fucking crazy. You've been since we were kids and I wouldn't have any other darkness in my life. When will you see that?" He tilts his head to the side.

Raising my hand, I touch the side of his face.

"I do now." The words come out of my mouth before I can catch them.

His lips crash into mine, and I accept graciously. The rough caress of his beard, his soft lips on mine, the taste of weed filling my mouth like I just took a fresh drag off a blunt.

The kiss is desperate, demanding, and locking me in as Benji's property for life. He doesn't say it, but I feel it. Then again, I've always been his.

His hands run up my sides with a greedy tendency, their rough and callused but in possessive need. They dig into my side hard, but the way they skirt all along my curves in a greedy manner I know it's his way of loving me. Years of pent-up sexual tension releasing at once. He opens the door to his car and shoves me in the back seat. The familiar smell of leather and weed comforting me. Climbing in after me, he shuts the door and slides in between my legs. He's so big he takes up most of the back seat. The top of his dark hair brushes against the headliner as he raises the dainty dress above my head, and rips the white panties from my waist in one tug. The cracks in the leather seat pinch my bare ass, but I could care less right now.

My hands lower, recklessly trying to pull off his skull belt. His lips continue to kiss every inch of my neck, a burn setting my skin ablaze from the scruff on his cheeks.

"Tell me something," he rasps.

"Hmm?" I lick my lips, tugging down his zipper.

"Did you never give me my ring back because you couldn't get it off or because it reminded you of me?" He lifts his chin, his blue eyes darker than ever.

I lift my hand and pull the ring off my thumb with ease. He reaches for it and I pull it out of his reach.

"I could get it off that night. I wanted it because when I look at it, I think of that night," I explain.

"Fuck, I love you," he groans, smashing his lips to mine. His tongue slides against mine, his mouth moving against mine in hunger. Our breaths depending on another to breathe.

Using my feet, I shove his jeans down to his knees. His lips trail down my chin, and my neck. His teeth biting my collarbone. My hands palm his head as he licks and nibbles my body, winding me up in a bundle of nerves.

"Do you touch yourself, Harley?" he asks against my nipple, his breath tickling me.

I glance down at him with confusion His eyes meet mine, his tongue flicking the rose bud of my tit.

"Do you climax thinking of me?" he clarifies.

I shift in the leather seat, my eyes avoiding his. How did he know I masturbated?

"Yes," I murmur embarrassed.

"Don't be ashamed, I jacked off to you daily. Sometimes twice a day," he reveals. I giggle.

"Really?"

"Fuck yeah, I can't get enough of you, baby." He dives his tongue into my belly button and my skin heightens to an all new level.

"Benji, I can't take anymore," I beg him to take me already. I've had to battle my inner feelings for him for years and I can't take another second of waiting. His hand slides down my leg, hooking it around his waist. He kisses my inner thigh before tugging with his teeth.

"You ready?"

I nod, my breathing so harsh I feel like I'm not breathing at all. With one jerk of his hips, his cock finds my heat. My head lolls back into the seat, his dick stretches me wide. Parting my mouth, I whimper in response. My nails digging into his back until they draw blood.

Just as he's seated, he stills. His eyes digging into mine.

"What?" I smile, and his lips pull into a sexy smirk.

"This is where I belong, I want to wake up every day and fuck you. Fall asleep every night with my dick inside of you."

Emotions fill my chest and I have to keep from crying.

We're made for each other. I cannot believe I fought it for so long.

Grasping my tit with one hand, his silver rings sparkle under the streetlight just outside. After I took his, the club gave him another one. He rocks into me with one quick drive of his hips, the feeling of pleasure and pain dancing inside of my core. It feels good, but it hurts at the same time. I'm pushing him away and pulling him close all at the same time.

One foot on the dash, the other on the headrest of the driver seat I try to widen my legs to accommodate him better. He's so big it's a tight squeeze in the one seat for the both of us.

"Promise me you'll never run again," he demands into the crook of my neck. His hot breath sticky on my neck.

"I promise," I relent, giving myself to him fully. If I run, we run.

Resting on his elbows, he looks into my eyes and presses something to my lips. I furrow my brows until the familiar feeling of my medication summons me. He brought my pills. I open my lips and take it.

"Swallow baby," he breathes heavily, and I do. My eyes flicking between his blue orbs. The pills dry in my throat, I cough them down.

"Do you have sex with Farrah too? Do you make love to her like you do me?" I can't help but ask.

His hand caresses my collarbone. "Like I said, Harley, Farrah is you and one day you will see that. I can't love you without loving her, baby." He shrugs, pumping in and out of me. Hearing that stings. I don't care if it's me, it doesn't feel like it's me.

Still, most men wouldn't fuck with my kind of crazy. For Benji to love all of mine, and want to help me, to chase me across the states... it's more than any man I've ever known to do for his girl.

My heart begins to break realizing how much Benji really cares for me. He tracked me down, found me, and has always taken care of me. Loving me no matter what I've done or who I may think I am.

His fingers intertwine between mine, holding them captive above my head. He slows his rhythm and everything becomes sensitive, softer.

My entire lower half buzzes with desire, I feel everything. In and out, in and out, his dick slides with ease. My wetness coating his cock as he pushes me to the brink of oblivion.

His lips purse into the shape of an O, just as my body warms into a ball of tingles. The car rocks back and forth, the windows now fogged from our hard breathing.

"Oh my God," I stutter out just as I'm about to come, he stops. My head whips up off the seat.

"Why'd you stop?" I breathe heavily.

"Be my ol' lady, Harley," he insists rather than asks, his breath hot and sticky against my neck. I still. Being Benji's ol' lady is not a question to ask lightly. It means I'm his club wife until he releases me. It means I'm patched in as his woman forever.

I'll have a cut, the club's colors on my back.

He growls, jerking his hips just right. I moan as I'm sensitive down there, my eyes rolling into my head. He's teasing me.

"Is this an ultimatum? Be my ol' lady or I'll hold your orgasm hostage?"

"Fucking straight. You say you're mine right now, or you'll never come. I'll hold your release hostage until you're on your knees begging me to fulfill your needs."

I bite my bottom lip to keep from smiling. Bad Benji is sexy.

"One day, Harley, I'm going to be at the head of that table, and I want you standing behind me at every meeting. That is your place in the club," he informs me with a firm voice.

I pull away from him, my eyes searching his for an explanation on how he's going to take the gavel from my father.

"How are you going to do—"

"Just fucking say yes," he demands, his fingers threaded with mine tightening.

"You promise?" I ask with sincerity.

"Promise what?" He tilts his head to the side, his dark hair falling in his eyes.

"That I'll be standing behind you at every meeting?"

He smirks, his charming smile causing my pussy to soak his cock still inside of me.

"I promise," he insists.

Taking my hand from his, I place it on the back of his neck and dig my nails in so deep his eyes narrow in on me.

"If you break my heart," my eyes bounce between the both his blue ones, "I will fucking kill you," I promise.

Raising his hands, he jerks my nails out of his skin and slams them down on my chest.

"The only one who is going to be doing heart breaking... is you. I've been chasing you ass for far too long to just walk away." He gives the side of my thigh a firm slap, and I swear my heart just pounded a little harder.

Looking up through my dark hair, I can't help the smirk tugging at my swollen lips. "I'll be your ol' lady," I whisper.

"I feel like there's a 'but' hanging off the tip of your tongue," he breathes heavily, his lips brushing mine. Raising his hand, his finger slides back and forth along my chin softly.

"But...You have to let me finish what I've started here," I compromise. I can't just walk away. I need to prove I can do this. To myself if anyone.

He stills, his fingers on my jaw.

"That professor is a dead man, Harley," he threatens, his tone savage and cold. "He touched what's mine, and if anything, his father-in-law owes the club."

I laugh, twirling my fingers in his hair.

"I was thinking the same thing." I bat my eyes.

His ass cheeks clench together as he pounds into my pussy. My eyes roll, my foot kicks the ceiling and my body comes alive in his hands on demand.

"Come on my dick now Harley," he commands, before smashing his lips to mine. Weed, whiskey, and everything that is Benji fills my senses. His mouth against mine causes my whole body to become sensitive and I combust into ecstasy. He picks up his pace, and before I can get another moan in, warm, thick liquid fills me just as I combust into a million little fucked up pieces.

Swirling his hips one last time, I shiver with satisfaction. My lungs burn needing air, and my back is sweaty and sticking to the leather seat from our hot breathing.

Pulling out of me, he sits up in the seat.

"Oh, Harley?"

"Yeah?" I ask breathily.

"If you ever run from me again. I will fucking kill you myself."
He looks over his shoulder at me with unforgiving eyes. He gave
his heart to me, and I will die with it before he lets me walk away
with it.

"That's the first rule of being my ol' lady."

16

FARRAH

Waking up, my body feels abused and used in the most satisfying of ways, and my thighs are so sore I can barely move them. I sit up and notice I'm naked. In bed. Warm, hot skin touches my side and my head whips in the direction of a man. Not just any man, but Benjamin.

I hold my head, the last thing I remember is me getting angry at the professor. Thinking about him makes hurt and fury resurface.

I sigh, whipping the covers off me. This wakes him.

"Harley?" he groans, half asleep.

"Good morning, Benjamin," I say in a less than welcoming way. If he thinks I'm going back with him, he has another thing coming.

"Farrah," he growls into the pillow. A puzzled expression wrinkles my face, curious how he knew it was me before he even lifted his head from the pillow.

"How'd you know it was me?"

"Only you call me Benjamin," he replies tiredly.

"What else would I call you?" I scoff.

"Harley calls me Benji. Only she can call me that too," he

clips. It's statements like that, that make me think he cares for her more than me.

"Hmm, I'm going to be late," I mumble, tucking my hair behind my ear.

"Farrah," he says my name as if he's angry. I turn, looking at him. He's propped up on his elbows, his hard chest shirtless and covered in skull tattoos.

"What?" I snap, my hand on my hip. His face wrinkles in anger and he climbs off the bed. His morning wood swings freely. I take a step back, my body pressing against the wall behind me. I know this game, he's going to fuck me against this wall, and I'll be satisfied and Harley will come forward.

Well, not this time.

Glaring down at me, he fists my ass cheek. I wince, my butt feels bruised. I look down and notice red prints on my backside. *Where the hell did those come from?*

He breathes on my neck, and I feel myself opening up to him. No. I press my palms against his bare chest, pushing him back.

"I was wondering when you'd come to save your damsel in distress," I sass, and his chest tenses beneath my palm. I struck a nerve.

"I like what you did to Harley's hair," he compliments. "The darkness suits—"

"*My* hair." I correct him.

He sighs, turning around. I can't help but look at his hard ass. You could bounce a quarter off that thing.

My eyes catch scratch marks down his back and I furrow my brows. I know we didn't have sex, so who'd he fuck?

"You should have called me when you came to the light, Farrah," he snaps, the playfulness in his voice gone. I've had sex with Benjamin a couple of times, but I was desperate for a man's touch, paired with his refusal to let me sleep with anyone other than him. Otherwise, I'd have Viper wrapped around my finger.

"Why, so you and Harley can out me?" I sneer, grabbing a lilac dress from the closet. I'm surprised Harley didn't burn these when she had the chance.

"Harley has never been to school, you guys shouldn't be here," he growls, his thick brows pulled inward with concern. He's right, Harley and I never went to school, how could we with our condition. I have to say though, I'm loving it here. We really missed out on a lot of things.

"Relax, I've been here most of the time and I must say it hasn't been all bad." I wink. Just thinking about all the things the professor and I did sends a tingle in between my thighs.

"You have a ... thing for the professor, don't you?" he says with a jealous tone.

I look over my shoulder with a devilish smile.

"Aww, Benjamin are we jealous?" I tease.

"It's not what Harley would want," he says confidently. He knows her so well as if he doesn't know me at all. It stings really, yet this game of defiance is so fun I can't help but make him chase me. Maybe one day he'll stop making Harley take those pills and I will be here permanently. We can run away together to a resort on a beach. Fuck all day and make love all night.

"Well, good thing I'm not Harley," I reply, grabbing for the concealer to cover up the tattoos on my arms.

A hand suddenly grips my wrist, stopping me. The touch hard and firm.

"But aren't you?"

My eyes slowly rise to his. He knows I hate it when he refers to me as Harley. I'm not her. She's... biker trash, a hood rat thug, and I'm... classier than that. I have ambition.

"When exactly did you come about, Farrah?" he asks with a tilted head, his voice laced with tension. Him questioning my existence angers me.

I snatch my hand from his. Ever since he came along, he's been trying to control me, make me his and I hate it.

"Why does it matter? I'm here, nothing you can do about

that..." I purse my lips.

"Is it because of her mother?" He ignores my taunting. "That's the only thing I don't know about Harley is when it comes to her mom. She shuts down whenever I ask, or smiles and acts like everything was perfect growing up."

I laugh so hard I double over. I'm suddenly slammed against the wall, and my laugh fades.

"I swear to God, if Harley wasn't in there somewhere I'd kill you right here," he seethes.

"Tell me something about Harley's mother and now. I'm fucking sick of not getting answers and the way you just laughed... I can tell you know something," he growls in my face, and my stomach knots, a cold sweat breaking down my spine. I've never seen Benjamin so angry before. Turning my head, I bite my bottom lip. Contemplating telling him anything about Harley's mother, after all, her mother is why I was created.

A little girl abused and neglected so her mother could get her rocks off in the other room. Taunted and ridiculed because a six-year-old wasn't doing tricks for money and helping pay rent.

Harley's mother resented everything she was, and the only way that little girl could keep the innocence about her... was me.

He gives me a curt shake, jostling the breath from my lungs.

"Harley's mother was anything but perfect," I finally spill, my eyes meeting his. "She was a whore, but wanted Harley to be more of a girl and less like... her dad," I breathe as if a weight had been released from my chest.

"That's when you were made... to cope with her mother," he mumbles under his breath. My heart beats faster that he put two and two together so quickly. "I can only imagine the shit that was done to her for you to be made." He shakes his head, his eyes looking at me with annoyance.

"She doesn't remember much of it, but what she does might have something to do with why she tries so hard to defy her feelings for you." I shrug, just pulling shit from the air now.

Letting go of me, I rub my throat and stare at him with curious eyes.

"You need to take your meds," he insists, snatching orange bottles off the desk beside the bed. Anger boils beneath the surface that he wants me out of here just when I got here.

Grabbing my backpack off the chair, I roll my eyes.

"Yeah, I'll get right on that."

"She's going to kill him, you know. You're wasting your time," he informs bitterly. I stop, my fingers tickling the doorframe as I stare at a naked Shadow Keeper in my dorm room. "I'll kill him," he threatens, talking about the professor. "You may think you're not mine, but think again."

The vindication in his tone brings goosebumps racing along my skin.

"I have no doubt you two will kill him. That's what you do," I whisper, Harley and him have been partners in crime since I can remember.

I look over my shoulder just now putting two and two together that I was naked and sore between the thighs when I woke up, and Benjamin is still naked. Harley slept with him! She gave in. My eyes widen with realization, confusion rocking my brain. What does this mean?

My heart flutters in my chest, a dark relenting feeling filling my stomach. If Harley can love, will I still be around?

"Are you and Harley together?" I can't help but ask.

A Cheshire Cat grin plasters across his face.

"Yeah, and now that she's mine, I'm going to see to it that she's taking her meds and gets better. You won't be running the show at all," he warns.

I bite my inner cheek until blood draws. Benjamin and Harley were made for each other, now it's time for me to find my soulmate... before they kill him.

Jerking the door open, I saunter out with sadness and longing heavy in my chest. If Harley is coming to terms with her side of love, I may not be around much longer.

"Get back here, Farrah!" he demands, running out into the hallway naked. He holds his cock, looking at me like he wants to kill me. But he can't because he's naked and stuck in the hallway.

"You don't get to dictate my life, Benjamin."

Walking to class, the warm sun shines down on my bare shoulders causing my dress to stick to my sweaty thighs from the unbearable heat. It's going to be a hot one today.

Keeping my head down, I silently wonder if Professor Prescott will be more open with me today. We didn't leave on the best of terms yesterday. I wonder if he's even alive.

"Farrah!"

My brows furrow from the female voice, did someone just say my name?

"Harley Vander!" That catches my attention, and I stop where I'm standing.

Turning I find June, the professor's wife, trying to catch up to me in the mix of college students. She stands out like a sore thumb amongst college football shirts and beanies, in her white ruffled blouse, black slacks, and black high heels. Her hair is pinned up in an up-do making her look professional, but sultry at the same time. She has it all, no wonder Michael is holding on to her.

"Yes?" I ask with a smile.

"Do you have a minute?" She presses her hands together, her face awkward as if she's afraid I'll say no. Her face is flawless, not a zit or scar anywhere.

"For?"

"I just, I needed to ask you a few things and was hoping—"

"I'll be late for class." I point to professor's class just over my shoulder. A few more feet and I can smell pencil shavings and permanent marker.

"It won't be but a minute, promise?" She smiles politely. Her teeth so white they're near blinding. Talking to her is growing tension in my shoulders, I mean she's the wife of the man I was trying to sleep with after all. "Please?" Her begging is beneath her and piques my curiosity.

Sighing I nod. "Sure."

I follow her across the yard to a tall stone building, once inside the air conditioning is on blast and my skin pebbles with goosebumps from the sweat trickling down my calves. My dress feels damp and my hair sticks to my flushed face.

June looks perfect though, not a drop of sweat on her. I furrow my brows noticing I'm jealous of her.

Her heels click amongst the marble flooring as we wind down a hallway with abstract paintings on the walls.

"This way," she informs, opening the door.

Stepping inside her office, there's a desk to the left with a computer and small bonsai tree. A purple chair is sitting across from the desk, and a side table holds a box of sand with a rake. It smells of sandalwood in here too, or is that lavender? Either way, it's very relaxing.

"Have a seat," she gestures to the purple chair.

"I'll stand," I retort nicely. I don't feel comfortable in here or with her. I doubt anything she has to say will be good.

There's a bunch of bookshelves behind the purple chair and I take it upon myself to look at them.

"I'll just cut to the chase, then. Are you sleeping with my husband?" she blurts. I smile wolfishly, my fingers tickling the spines of thick doctor books. Nothing I would ever read, I'm more of a horror fan myself.

"Does that bother you?" I question, it's a stupid question really. *Does that bother you?* Of course, it would.

"Oh, please, honey, if you think you're the only hussy I've had to chase off, then you're dumber than I thought," she laughs, and my spine stiffens hearing I'm not special. I knew I wasn't but to hear her say it... it's nails on a chalkboard. I turn, glaring at her.

"I'm just curious how bad it is *this time*. Does he have you in an expensive apartment somewhere?" She sizes me up and I feel like I'm suddenly naked in front of her. "I don't see any expensive rings on your fingers, promising you he'll leave me, so that's a plus sign." Her eyes settle on mine, blue dominating eyes tearing me apart. "It can't be that serious then, huh?"

I sit in the chair, my heart beating so fast I feel sick. If the girl in the painted overalls wasn't a hint that her husband sleeps around, this is.

"So he does this often?" How can she be with a man that does this over and over to her? The idea I'm just another plaything to him, another notch on his belt if I were to sleep with him hits me in all the wrong places, so how can she be so okay with it? Does she sleep around too?

Either way, Professor Michael Prescott is a dirtbag. He broke my heart and will pay the price.

"Yes, and no matter what he says... he's never left me. For anyone." She tilts her head to the side, looking at me with sympathy. I don't like the way she's looking at me as if I'm beneath her.

My eyes sting, threatening with tears to rush down my face.

"I'm so stupid!" I grit through clenched teeth, anger rattles my chest. I fell hook line and sinker for a tool.

"By the way, I tried to pull up your file in the school database, and there's nothing on you except a name, Harley Vander. Why is that? And why do you choose to go by Farrah?" She clicks on her computer with a confused look, but I ignore her. All I can think about is that scum bag professor cheating on his wife with tons of college girls. Holding girls up in expensive apartments, giving them fine diamonds with empty promises. *Why didn't he do this for me?*

I'm so upset, so angry I can feel Harley cussing inside my head. There's no confining her I'm so emotional this time, and to be honest. I don't want to. I want her to fuck this place up.

I want her to hurt the professor like he's done me.

17

HARLEY

Blinking, a room comes into view, beside me a box of sand with a fork looking tool. My head feels heavy and foggy, the cries of Farrah echoing in my head.

"Farrah?" My head snaps forward and I see June. My fucking target sitting right in front of me.

My heart skips a beat and my nails dig into my palm with a sudden rage.

"I mean, there are no hard feelings. If anything, I should be thanking you for keeping Michael out of my hair." She giggles and I see what's going on here. She's confronting Farrah for her crush on the professor.

I stand, slowly walking to her. "Stop playing your games. Your husband is an asshole who thinks he can take advantage of young women. That there are no consequences to sticking his dick wherever he wants because he's not getting ass at home. He's a manipulative pervert and for you to know about his transgressions and to still be with him, it says a lot about who you are. You're as bad as him." I don't hold back. Her face frowns, brows furrowing in.

"Careful or you'll get frown lines," I taunt, pointing to her face.

"Farrah." She clears her throat, her face turning red as I insult her. I'm not saying Farrah was in the right trying to sleep with her man, but bringing Farrah here only to get in her head and hurt her... is not going to fly. No one fucks with Farrah without getting repercussions I will bring.

"My name is Harley," I insist, and her face goes blank with confusion. "Is your dad the governor?" I ask, just to make sure I'm not mistaken who she is.

"Yes, I've told you that, but I don't see what that has to do with anything we're speaking of," she scoffs. She didn't tell me that, she must have told Farrah that. Next to her computer, I see a pair of sharp scissors and I grab them. She stands with panic in her eyes.

"Farrah, please." Her hands come up in a defensive manner. "I know Michael needs help, and bringing you in here to release my problems wasn't right. I see that now." She scrambles for an excuse for me to spare her.

Carefully, I step around her desk and like a snake, I whip out and grab her by the throat. Her skin isn't as soft as I thought it would be. Too many chemicals and toxic lotions. She cries, and I press the scissors into her neck. One jeer and it will puncture the main artery causing her to bleed out in seconds.

"Shut up, or I'll cut you. Do you understand?" I whisper. She rolls her lips onto one another, tears streaming down her smooth cheeks as she nods. "I want you to call your husband and tell him to meet you at the house. Do you understand?"

"Yes," she sobs, snot dripping from her nose as she breathes hard. I breathe in her fear, and it rushes into my soul. The rush of having control is something I've sought for far too long.

Carefully she reaches for the phone on her desk and dials.

"Can – can you meet me at the house?" her voice trembles with fear, and I like it. Fear is respect in the eye of the club.

She looks at me and I tap the blade of the scissors on my chin in waiting.

"I know you're in a lecture, but it's ... it's an emergency goddamn it." She starts to become hysterical, and I shake my head in warning.

She glances at me again, her makeup starting to run down her face and show her acne scars. I begin to lose my patience and press the scissors to the back of her spine in hopes to hurry this the fuck up.

"JUST FUCKING DO IT, MICHAEL!" she hollers before hanging up.

"Good girl," I whisper. "Now, take me to your car and I swear to God, if you let on anything is going on, I will shove this into your spine. Do you understand?"

"Why are you doing this? Is it because of the affair?" she cries. "I don't care, he's just a front. I don't love him—"

I laugh. "Affair? Oh, no no no. This is because your greedy father owes my club money and until I figure out what I'm going to do about it. You and your shithead husband are mine."

She hangs her head. "Shit," she mutters in knowing.

"Ah, so you know Daddy is a dirty fucker?"

She responds with an angry glare.

"Where are you parked?"

"In the garage today, I didn't want the sun to fade the paint on the car." She goes into detail, and I could really care fucking less about her expensive ass car. I just need a getaway driver and she's it.

"Go," I push the blade into her back and she hisses, but walks forward. Keeping my arm close to her back I follow her out of her office, and up a flight of stairs to an elevator.

"You know, we can talk about this," she says over her shoulder as we wait.

"I'm more of a doer, not a talker," I reply calmly. "Does the professor have a way home?"

"He- he drove in today," she informs. Perfect.

The elevator doors open and we step inside, the sound of classical music playing. I hate this kind of music, it puts me to sleep. The scene is ironic really. Pretty rich girl with tears streaming down her cheeks, makeup melting down her face, and here I am standing behind her in a sweaty dress with a pair of sharp scissors pressed into her back while soothing music plays in the elevator.

The doors open and she walks out on shaky legs. Her heels clicking on the concrete until we reach a black Range Rover.

Reaching into her pocket, she pulls out her keys and unlocks it with a trembling hand. I slide into the back seat as she gets behind the wheel.

"It's not too late, we can—"

"DRIVE!" I press the scissors inside of her ear.

She cries out and fumbles with the keys to start the car. I can't help but smile. The fucking rush of having someone else's life in your hands is a high like no other.

If this is what the club does on a daily basis, I could easily get used to it.

18

BENJI

Looking out the window of the dorm room, I begin to worry. I shouldn't have let Farrah walk out of here. I should have stomped down the hall and pulled her back in this fucking room. Demanded she get her shit and leave. It's been hours since she left, and I'm starting to worry. If the Governor finds out what she's up to, he'll have her snatched. We should have never did business with that crooked fucker.Grabbing my phone, I try to dial her, but it goes to voicemail. Shit!

Sliding on my jeans and shirt, I grab my gun and slide it into my waistband. The hair on my neck stands on it as a cold chill rushes through the hot room. Something bad is going to happen tonight, I can feel it.

Whatever Harley had going on here. It's done. We're heading home.

Heading to the corner of her room I grab her leather bag, and a gun falls to the floor.

"What the fuck?" I crouch down, inspecting it.

On the side, the skull of the club is sketched in. It's one of the patched in brothers. Where the hell did she get this from.

Palming the gun, I remember my dad passing out drunk a few

years back and his gun went missing. He got a lot of prospect shit for losing that and had to pay for a new one.

I shake my head, tossing the gun back into her leather bag. She's going to turn this campus upside down.

I need to find Harley and now.

Stepping outside I head to the building of the professor and see a note stuck to the door saying class was canceled. I furrow my brows. *Where the fuck is Farrah then?*

A young kid walks out of the doors with the note on it. Holding my hand out, I stop him.

"Hey, where's the teacher at?"

"Some emergency, he just went home." The boy looks me up and down, fear striking in his eyes of who the fuck I am, and I release him.

"Fuck," I mutter under my breath.

If Farrah has him, they're fucking and he's a dead man.

If Harley has him, he's still a dead man.

Either way, he's dead.

19

HARLEY

June drives out of the college parking lot and sobs the whole time. Her stereo playing a CD of how to cope with not loving your spouse. This couple has major problems.

"Jesus, turn that shit off." I wave the scissors towards the stereo. Her fingers stab at the dash until the sound of the woman's clinical voice cuts off.

Riding in silence I can't help but wonder why she's with the professor if she's so unhappy. Why not let him run off with Farrah or one of the other school girls?

"Why do you stay with him?" I can't help but ask.

Her shoulders rise as she inhales a shaky breath.

"It's a long story," she murmurs under her breath.

"I like long stories," I lie. I'm more intrigued by other humans and the stupid things they do.

She takes a left, the car hitting a pothole causing the scissors to press into her head a little harder than I intend.

She hisses grabbing at her hurt ear.

"Shit sorry," I mutter, and I pull them back.

"He was the cute new guy at the college, and I had just started volunteering there. We hooked up in the library one night after classes were over, and six weeks later I found out I was pregnant."

She looks in the rearview mirror, her eyes holding more sadness in them than I've seen before. Now I just feel sad for her.

"My dad demanded he marry me as he didn't want our family name to be mocked as he ran for governor."

"Dads can be controlling," I speak from experience.

"You have no idea," she scoffs.

"Story for another time," I clip, resting in the back seat comfortably. This car is nice, nicer than anything I've been in before. I slide my hand along the smooth leather wondering if I'll ever have a car like it. A baby to sit in the back seat. If I'll play house with Benji.

"So, you got knocked up and married an asshole?" I look back at her, wondering if her story is over.

"I lost the baby and am stuck with the asshole. Michael knows too much of what my father does for my dad to let him walk away." She shakes her head, and the ride to her house falls silent.

It'd be easy for me to tell her what I would do, but I know what it's like living a life of crime and secrets.

You have no life. Your life becomes the sin and secrets, they run the river of darkness around your little happiness.

June drives her Range Rover into the garage of her house and places it in park. Looking out the tinted back seat window it looks as if she just moved in. There's no tools on the wall, a workbench or anything of lawn maintenance. The garage is clean, not even a grease stain on the floor.

"Did you just move here?" I can't help but ask.

"No, I just... I don't like clutter," she replies with a raspy voice, her silky hands white-knuckling the steering wheel. Oh, I bet she's a peach to live with. If she saw my room at the club, she'd pass out.

"Hmm," I smile. "Get out." I tap her head with the scissors

and she whimpers before fumbling with the door handle. She scares easily, I like it.

Getting out, she stands there looking at me as if she's lost. Like a kid dropped off at daycare for the very first time.

"Well, let's go inside?" I prompt her with irritation laced in my voice.

She tucks a strand of hair behind her ear and heads to a white door on the left. Stepping inside the house we walk into an immaculate kitchen. The hardwood floors are clean without so much as a single scratch marking them, and the marble counters are clear of any cooking utensils or food. She must have some OCD or something as I've never seen a place so clean. Then again, I live with a bunch of bikers.

My eyes fall on the one thing on the counter next to the stove; a knife block with tall sharp looking knives. I glance at my current weapon. I should upgrade. I can't believe this, I have a gun back in my dorm room. With the scissors pointing at her, I head to the knives and grab the biggest one out of the wooden block. The blade scratches amongst the block as I release it from its holding. It's so clean and shiny I can see my reflection clearly in it.

"Sit!" I demand, pointing to a high back chair next to a long wooden dining table.

She heads over to the chair and sits down, her legs crossed. I run my hands along the back of one of the chairs. It's covered with cloth, not like the metal chairs at the club.

"This is nice," I admire. Soft too. It looks like something that would belong at a vanity rather than a kitchen table.

"Th-thanks." She gives me a weak smile. I can tell she doesn't want to be nice to me, and I don't blame her for it.

"You don't have to be fake with me, you won't offend me. In fact, it's the fake people that don't scare me, it's the genuine ones. They're the ones that slip past your walls and get close to you. Loyal people know your weakness," I state from experience. Benji, he's the one person that scares the shit out of me because he knows me so well. Ones like him get caught in a web of passion that have you not walking away from them so easily.

I start rummaging through drawers looking for something to tie June up with when I hear her clear her throat.

"You don't have to do this. Nobody has to get hurt," she implores with a whiny voice. I chuckle, as I pull open another drawer. *Duct tape, bingo!* We use this for everything at the club.

Grabbing it, I head over to her fancy ivory chair.

"Sit back," I instruct, and she quickly obeys. Placing the knife in between my teeth, I snatch her hands up from her lap, placing her palm to palm before wrapping the tape around her wrists. When I'm done I place them back in her lap and then tape her body to the chair so she can't escape.

Done, I blow the hair from my face and look at my artwork.

"Aren't you going to tape my mouth?" she asks with confusion.

I raise a brow. "How are you going to call Daddy if I have your mouth taped shut?" I raise a brow. Her big blue eyes flash with panic before looking elsewhere.

My eyes skim down her frame, she's so in shape and pretty. She could have anyone, it's sad she has to try and love the man she's with. The risqué shoes on her feet grab my attention and I step closer to get a better look. They're black with red underneath them. Like the kind I see celebrities wearing in magazines. Not being able to leave the club much, Benji would bring me new magazines every month so I wouldn't be bored. I would scour the pages circling things I'd love to wear, or have one day and those black shoes... was one of the things I've circled a few times. I'm not much for heels, but those are just so damn sexy I'd pet them every day in my closet. Bending over, I grab one and jerk it from her foot.

"What size are you?" I question, looking the shoe over. It's a

Jimmy Choo, it must have cost a fortune. "I've never worn heels before," I say more to myself than her, but she doesn't respond.

"Take them, you- you can have them," she insists with vulnerable eyes. "I have a whole closet you can have if you let me go."

I roll my eyes at her, she can't buy me with shoes.

"Unless you have a closet full of leather boots, your ass is stuck in that chair," I inform her. I hold the shoe up. "This just happens to be the only kind of heel I'm interested in and not to wear."

She blinks a few times like I'm an idiot.

"You're not even going to wear them?"

"I mean, I might... I don't know," I shrug, looking the slick shoe over. I'd need to practice walking in them because knowing my luck I'd try and act sexy for Benji and fall on my face.

"Honey? Are you in here?" the panicked voice of Professor Prescott echoes through the house as he looks for his wife. I drop the shoe to the ground and quickly hide beside the fridge until he walks in. Knife in my hand I palm it tightly, my teeth clenched tightly as I wait for him to walk past.

"June?" He looks at his tied-up wife in confusion. I quietly step up behind him like a snake slithering up to his prey and pinch the spine of his back with the tip of the sharp knife.

"Don't fucking move!" I warn, and he freezes. His arms raise like I have a gun, and I smile. The scent of him whirls around me. Erasers, marker, and hand sanitizer. He smells what I would imagine a kindergarten room would smell like. It's repulsive. His hair is slicked back and his face is clean shaven like a baby's ass. What does Farrah see in this tool?

"Go sit beside your wife," I instruct, waving the knife toward June.

"Farrah... let's talk about this," he suggests with a calm voice. Like lightning, anger strikes my chest violently. I fist his hair with my free hand roughly, his neck popping with my harsh force.

"There's nothing to fucking talk about and stop calling me fucking Farrah. I'm Harley, understand?" I breathe into his ear.

"Okay, okay," he hisses with pain. I tug his hair one more time before I let go. Using my foot, I kick him in the back, shoving him forward.

"Move it!" I roar.

He rubs his back before stumbling over to the chair next to June.

"I can explain," he whispers to her.

"Save it." She rolls her eyes, looking the other way.

Grabbing the tape, I tape him up just like June. He sits there without a fight, looking at June with puppy dog eyes.

"Wow, not even going to try and fight me, huh?" I ask with surprise.

"I don't hit women," he sneers. He pulls his eyes away from his wife and looks up at me with defiant eyes.

"You pussy," I laugh, I was hoping he'd struggle just a little bit. I'd like to test out if I could take a man down or not. "You guys really are making this too easy."

"Is this about us because I thought I was—"

"Oh, shut up, Michael. This has nothing to do with you throwing your prick to easy college girls!" June screams, her face turning red. I stand back and cross my arms. I'm impressed she's standing up for herself. It's like a fucked-up version of couples counseling.

"What is that supposed to mean?" he acts offended.

"Oh, don't act like you haven't been trying to sleep with this girl." She tilts her head to the other side, the sight of Michael too much for her.

He looks up at me for a lifeline, for the poor man can't figure out why he and his pretend wife are tied to a chair.

"This has nothing to do with *you*, this has everything to do with June and her father though," I sigh, placing my hands on my hips. The professor looks at his wife with a blank stare.

"You're kidding," he mutters almost angrily.

"Daddy owes her club money," June shrugs.

He slumps against the chair and shakes his head.

"Go figure," he grumbles. His head snaps to my direction. "Then what does this have to do with me? Why am I here? I have nothing to do with her dad."

My mouth drops. "I don't know, I thought maybe you'd want to fight in your wife's honor, die together, some romantic crap." I swing the knife around as I explain my actions. To be honest, I wanted him here in-case I needed him for bait.

Crossing my arms, I tilt my head to the side and observe the two mysterious people in front of me.

"I bet if I let you go right now, you'd run and leave June behind. Wouldn't you?" I ask with curiosity. He glances at June before looking the other way. He would, he'd run and never look back. As if there was nothing between them, and they didn't create life together at one point. Even couples who divorce later keep a respectful relationship due to their past. At least, that's what I read in magazines.

"Wow, you really are a piece of shit." I'm astonished.

"That's not what you were saying the other day," he mocks. He must be talking about Farrah.

"Did we fuck?" I mindlessly ask, this grabs June's attention.

His eyes widen. "No, but I was going –"

June doesn't let him finish his sentence before she starts rocking her chair in his direction. Her teeth clashing and nostrils flaring with rage, she wants to claw his eyes out. She still loves him, if she didn't she wouldn't be so upset.

"Oh fuck off, if you weren't such a princess, maybe I wouldn't have to stick my dick somewhere else!" He rolls his eyes.

Before I know it, they're in a screaming match. Again.

Closing my eyes, I feel emotional, sad, and the voice of Farrah in my head. I turn, my hands grabbing at the air as I feel for the counter. My vision is blurring and my stomach coils into a tight knot.

"No, not now," I tell myself. It does no good, black begins to stain my vision. These two hurting inside and each other is making my emotions roll inside of me like an unstoppable tide.

Michael and June screaming at each other makes my head go foggy and I have to fall on top of the counter to keep from falling face first into it.

20

FARRAH

Coming to, I see before me June and Professor Prescott tied in chairs. I have tape in one of my hands, and a knife in the other. They're yelling at each other, completely oblivious to me being here.

Pulling myself off the counter, I look around noticing I'm in their house once again, it's so clean I feel dirty.

"You take advantage of young girls!"

"They want my dick! They want my affection. Unlike you! All you can think about is yourself!"

"Maybe if you actually had a dick, that would change! The only affection you have in your body is for the sight of money, and you know it!"

"Maybe if you would just let me love you, I wouldn't have to treat women like objects! Fucking girl from girl behind your back just to feel something inside. You think I like that?"

My heart constricts watching them fight. Hearing the professor refer to me as an object. I was his object. A toy.

"Is that what I was?" I interrupt as I look the knife in my hand over. They both shut up and look at me with wide eyes. "Was I just an object to you? Another cum dumpster waiting on the sidelines?" I quip with a light shrug. I play it off, but inside I'm cracking, I'm falling apart.

I can't tell if I'm sad or angry. I feel what I feel, hurt, but in the background, I hear Harley in my head screaming in anger at the professor. It causes my hand to shake, the knife in my hand a tempting tool to end the professor's game.

"We didn't fuck," he informs dryly. As if he didn't stick his penis in me we had zero connection; no feelings were involved. My eyes fall to the floor. Was everything in my head, was there never a connection. Maybe I wanted one so bad, I made it all up in my head.

"You told me you didn't love her, but you didn't want to love me either." I flick my eyes from the floor to him

"What did you expect, a diamond ring? You're not wife material, babe," he scoffs before crossing his shiny black shoes over one another. He sounds like one of the dumb boys at the college.

My heart falls to my feet in shards of heated passion. No one to love and nobody to care for me. Thunder claps against my rib cage as I try to breathe through the raging sea inside my chest. My palm begins to sweat as the knife in my hand burns into my skin. Voices in my head telling me to use it, to hurt him like he hurt me.

I drop it and gasp for air.

Looking up through my bangs, I cannot contain all of the feelings combusting in my chest like a giant firecracker going off on the Fourth of July. I run at him, tackling him to the ground. Falling to the floor the chair splinters into a million pieces.

June is screaming in fear and I'm so angry so sad and full of loneliness... I let the voices take over and the black bleeds into visions of chaos and blood.

Benji

PULLING up to the house of the professor I hear Harley screaming from inside. Slamming the car in park, I jump out, not bothering to shut the door behind me. Running across the lawn, I head inside the house with my gun drawn.

Stepping inside, my boots leave muddy prints behind, and I whip my gaze and gun to the left and right. Finding nothing, I head further into the house.

Coming into a kitchen, I find the governor's daughter tied up in a chair screaming as she rocks the chair back and forth. Right beside her on the ground is the professor tied up and trying to fight off Harley.

Harley. I let out a small breath seeing her alive. Beating the shit out of the professor, but alive. I lower my gun and head toward her.

Harley freezes from pummeling the teacher and grabs a high heel next to his head. I hurry to her just as she screams so loud my ears ring, and the point of the heel cracks into the side of his skull.

The sound of shoe and skull one I've not heard before I stop. My eyes flicking from Harley and the man on the ground. Did she kill him?

The professor stills beneath her, blood spilling from his head and filling the shoe.

"Fuck," I whisper under my breath.

"NOOOO!" June screams, her makeup and tears chapping her face. Rocking the chair hysterically, she tries to get to him. But it's too late, he's dead. The heel of the shoe is dug into his skull so far there's no pulling it out. Harley blinks a couple of times, her hands clasping the shoe. I know that look. She's just coming to, Farrah must have been in the light.

Wait? Did Farrah kill the professor? Shaking my head of the thought, I quickly rush over to her and gently lay my hand on hers holding the heel lodged in the man's head, urging her to let go of the shoe. She begins to shake, a whimper spilling from her lips as she looks upon the dead man.

"Did- did I kill him?" she whispers with a shaky voice.

"It doesn't matter. Just let go," I coax her. It was both of them, they both killed the professor. The first time ever that Farrah and Harley worked together.

She looks up at me with wide ocean colored eyes. Her green irises looking darker with her soul set in panic.

"No, I need to know. Did I?" she begs me to tell her what happened. "All I remember is my arm striking down as I blinked from the darkness." She begins to cry, piecing the puzzle back together.

"TELL ME!?" she demands in a hysterical voice. "This was supposed to be my kill, not Farrah's!

I snake my arms around her tightly, trying to contain her panic. Her head falls back, her eyes closed as she cries through her mental pain.

"You both did it, babe," I whisper to her. She falls silent in my hold and I squeeze her tighter. Fuck, to feel her against me and to know she is okay and safe... it's a fucking relief. Her skin is clammy, her heart racing so fast I'm surprised she's not passed out.

She looks up at me with tear-filled eyes. Blood smeared on her right cheek and a lost look gazing at me for help. When she comes forward from being in the light of Farrah, she's confused and vulnerable. Often times, dangerous. Only I can control her.

"Stay still," I tell her. My go-to phrase for warding off the echoes in her head, the guilt panging in her chest at what just happened.

"Can you feel my heart beat against your back?" I whisper softly. She closes her eyes and nods. Her wet lashes fluttering along her face. "Can you hear only my voice?"

"Yes," she murmurs, the hysteria in her voice slowly fading.

"The chaos and the voices can't be heard if you stay still and let me have you," I remind her, tugging her closer to my warm body.

She opens her eyes, her hands clasping my leather cut with a death grip.

"Benji? I love you," she reveals softly.

I freeze. The clocks in the room stop ticking and my lungs seize to take in air.

"What?" I ask. I heard her, but I need to hear it again. I've chased this woman far too long to hear her confession as a mere whisper.

"I love you," she repeats, this time with more strength than before.

"Fuck, I love you too," I breathe heavily. Grasping the nape of her neck, I take her lips to mine. The smell of blood, leather, and her scent of bubblegum filling my head.

Her lips a perfect match to mine, my hands pull her dainty dress over her head and throw it in the corner with reckless abandon. She wraps her legs around my waist and her lips eagerly kissing all over my neck. One of her hands slides along the wooden floor guiding her back to the floor, the other pulling me on top of her.

Her body is rushing with adrenaline and need. The rush to fuck and feel something rather than face what just happened her only mission.

My jeans a little loose, I shove them down to my ankles, and she tugs my briefs down far enough for my cock to spring free. It's hard and throbbing. Veins protruding around it and the pulsing sensation is so intense I'm ready to tear into her sweet pussy. I don't give a fuck if the wife tied to the chair is watching and there's a dead guy, feet away from us.

I'm taking her now.

Spreading her legs her sweet cunt drips, ready for me.

"Say it again?" I demand.

"I love you. Love me!" she pants, reaching forward she fists my cock and I thrust inside of her.

"Fuck yes." I push through gritted teeth. Propping myself on one elbow, I use my free hand to grasp her bare thigh, pulling her closer to me. Needing her skin touching my skin, wanting to feel her wrapped around me. Her pussy is tight and warm, it's like fucking heaven between her legs.

Anywhere else is hell and even though I'm a bad man... I'm not to her.

Her eyes are closed as she rocks back and forth on the cold floor with every thrust. Her cheeks flush, and hair of brown and pink splay around her like a dark angel.

"Excuse me?" the wife says with disgust. "Are you guys serious?"

"Shut up!" Harley yells, pleasure thick in her voice causing her to sound raspy.

Gently I cup her neck as my dick pulses inside of her. This bitch is mine, she said it herself. She gave herself to me, and my next step is going to be taking that fucking gavel from her old man.

She just doesn't know it yet.

Looking between our heated bodies, I watch as my cock slides in and out of her pussy lips. Her wetness coating my dick. Her pink cunt, squeezing, and milking my length so fucking good.

"You like that cock?"

"God, yes." She rocks against me.

Her face scrunches, her body tensing as she's about to come. Her fiery eyes look up at me, her mouth parting as she tenses beneath me. The sight of her coming undone unravels me and I swirl my hips as I rock into her harder. My cock pumping every drop of cum I have to offer right inside of her.

Out of breath, she looks directly at me. Her chest rising and falling with rapid breaths. Her tongue slides along her lips, wetting them.

She glances at the wife and her cheeks turn the brightest shade of red from embarrassment. So lost in the moment, she didn't really think about fucking in front of a stranger.

Quickly, she uses her elbows to sit up, shyness creeping into her eyes. I shimmy off my cut to help cover her and to keep her warm, as I lean over and grab her dress I threw in the corner.

Pulling my jeans up, I risk taking a glance at the wife. She's so red in the face it's humorous.

"Sorry, we could have fucked in your bed, but when the moment hits... it hits," I chuckle.

"Brother?" Harley and I look to a familiar voice.

Viper stands in the doorway with a gun in his hand, looking like the fucking police. His blonde hair a mess as if he's been running his hands through it anxiously. He's wearing his cut and a black shirt with holes all in it. His jeans the same.

"What the fuck are you doing here?" My brows furrow in question.

He whips his gun in my direction and when he sees me, his shoulders relax and he lowers the .45.

"Fuck, man." He's angry. "I've been trying to call you. You had me scared to death something fucking happened!"

"How'd you find us?" Harley asks, standing up. Now fully dressed.

He points to me. "Dipshit's, phone." I scowl at him. He looks down at the dead body and then to June. "Fuuuck." He looks amused. His eyes bloodshot and dilated from drugs.

"Seriously, why are you here?" I ask again.

He shakes his head, his hand raising to rub at his chin.

"Word has it you went rogue, brother. Grudge is telling everyone you went against code and shit. I knew it wasn't true, so I had to find you, make sure you were still breathing."

Biting my bottom lip, I point at him at a loss for words. Grudge is going against me and it stings.

"It's not true," I clip. Raising my hand, I rub at my chin, staring Viper down. He has to know I would never turn my back on my club. Grudge, yes, but not my club. Grudge is playing a dangerous game trying to throw me under the bus. He wants to get rid of me because he wants to get rid of Harley because she's a threat to him. But with me around, that will never happen.

"My dad... he's forgotten the creed of our club," Harley whispers, the sadness in her voice makes my chest constrict. She's tough, but I hate that she has to be that way.

I raise a brow and rub the back of my neck as I look the group over. "We'll deal with him when we get back to the club."

"What are we going to do with her?" Viper asks, nodding his head at June.

Looking at her, I exhale a deep breath. Taped to the chair she continues to look at her dead husband, the high heel still sticking out of his head morbidly.

"Use her as bait," Harley insists, her voice now with confidence. "Her dad did fuck us over, you already got this far, might as well play it out, babe." I approve. Harley needs this. She needs to see what we do on runs, see if this is where she wants her place in the club to be.

Harley steps over to the professor and digs in his pocket a second before pulling out a black phone. Her hand shakes, and she keeps her head as far away as she can from the dead body. I can tell just by looking at her, she's not ready for this kind of shit. She wants to be a part of the club, but when it comes to this shit... she's not going to be around it. Not if I can help it.

I know she won't sit behind the counter and sling drinks to the boys, and I don't want her to, but I also don't want bloodshed on my woman's hands. She deserves better than that.

"What are you doing with that?" Viper looks confused.

Ignoring Viper, Harley takes a picture of the scene before us. June taped to a chair, her hair and face a fucking wreck. A broken chair splintered all over the floor next to her, and her husband dead in a cold pool of blood. A black and red heel sticking out of his skull. His eyes are open and mouth agape.

It's pretty fucking gruesome looking.

The clicking noise makes June look away and she continues to weep.

"I sent the picture to the contact governor, texted him told him to pay up or she's next. He'll know who he needs to pay," she informs, handing me the phone.

My mouth goes slack with the wits of this bitch, she's constantly surprising me. I put it in my pocket and run my hand over my sweaty forehead.

"I bet he owes a lot of people money," Viper scoffs, crossing his arms.

"This is fucking ridiculous," June huffs. "How much could he possibly owe for you to do something like this?" Her wide glossy eyes fall to each one of us. "You're all animals. Fucking animals!" She begins to lose her shit.

"Doesn't matter how much he owes, it's about the respect." My tone dry.

She rolls her eyes, tears streaming down her cheeks. Turning away from her I look to Viper.

"Until the dad pays up, take my car, Harley, and this bitch back to the club. I have a mess to clean up," I inform. In a neighborhood like this, it's only a matter of time before someone gets nosy and calls the cops.

"Wait, you want me to go without you?" Harley looks at me with confusion wrinkling her face. Her eyes wide, and mouth parted beautifully. I don't want to be away from her either, but it's safer this way.

"Yes, it's not safe. The governor could retaliate or the cops could show up. I want you at the club. I'll be there soon after." I toss her my keys and she catches them with confused eyes. "Follow Viper back to the club."

"What about my stuff at the dorm?"

"You mean your gun?" I glower at her, and her face falls.

"I'll get everything. Nobody will know you were even there," I tell her. I'm not good at a lot of shit, but making people disappear is one thing I excel in.

"But this is my mess, I should help," Harley insists, ignoring June.

Grabbing her by the neck, I kiss her on the forehead.

"I've been cleaning up your messes since we were kids, Harley."

21

BENJI

Wiping my forehead with the back of my hand, I drop the shovel to the mound of freshly patted dirt and fall to my ass. Out of breath and shirt sticking to my sweaty chest, I pull my top off and throw it to the side.

"Fuck, it's hot." Digging in my back pocket, I pull out a smashed joint. With everything that has happened in the last twenty-four hours, I need something to take the edge off. Licking my fingertips, I try and straighten it back out as much as I can. The smell of skunk and green making my mouth water, I light the fucker and rip the biggest drag from it and blow it into the night sky. Falling back on the grave of the professor, I look at the stars.

Me as the president of the Shadow Keepers. I smile, the image of Harley by my side as I sweep the streets of Arizona with sin and respect. Moods will rise and dark waters will pass when I take the gavel. Taking another drag, I sit up. The desert bare of any life, no animals, no brush. It's just dry fucking ground.

Things are about to get a lot fucking better, at least they will be when I eliminate Grudge. If none of my brothers have the balls to do it, I will. Standing with hazy eyes, I grab the shovel and head over to June's Range Rover. I'm going to drive it back to the club and strip it of any evidence before having it crushed.

Climbing inside her car, that stupid self-help CD starts playing again.

"Jesus, shut the fuck up!" I slam at the buttons on the dash until the radio kicks on. "Thunder" from Imagine Dragons fills the speakers. I prefer something a little heavier, but this will do for now. Better than that shit before.

Taking the back roads my eyes bounce between the windshield and the rearview mirror, smoking that joint has me paranoid as fuck that a cop is going to catch me in a stolen vehicle with blood-stained clothes. My nails are caked with dirt and the smell of metallic is strong. I'm so ready for a hot shower and my bed with a naked Harley smelling of bubblegum. Her pink nipples pressing into me and wetness rubbing on my thigh as I keep her warm. Shifting in my seat, I situated my dick, and take a breath.

I got a lot more shit to do before that can happen though.

A car just ahead stops, it's taillights illuminating the empty road. A nervous sweat beads my forehead. What if it's a cop.

"Calm the fuck down," I tell myself. This Range Rover being nicer than anything I've ever driven and doesn't help with my discomfort. Leather everywhere, the smell of new car scent making me sick. I've never been in something so expensive in my life. Big ass motherfucker like me in the front seat is a dead giveaway I stole this damn thing.

Driving past the stopped car, which is not a cop, I exhale a large breath.

Needing a better distraction, I flip the radio until a decent song comes on. "Nightmare" by Avenged Sevenfold plays and I thumb my fingers against the steering wheel. Now we're talking.

FINALLY PULLING up to the club, a prospect sits outside with a beer in his hand talking to Tickles. She's wearing a corset and shorts that could pass as underwear. She looks like a hooker hanging by the street. Hanging out the window, I wave my hand to get his attention.

"Open the garage!" I demand.

Noticing my eagerness, he runs to the garage and pulls the door open. The tires squeal as I pull it inside and turn the engine off.

"Where did you find this!" The prospect looks at the Range Rover with admiration. Dumb fuck wouldn't know what a good-looking car was if it ran over him. My El Camino is better in my opinion.

"Don't let anyone in here," I instruct him. Milking his beer, his eyes fuck the expensive car.

"You got it," he nods.

Heading inside the clubhouse, the wind shifts, and my spine stiffens. Viper is sitting at the bar with an icepack on his head, the back of his shirt spattered with blood. Grudge sits beside him drinking a beer, his green eyes darker than ever as he glares at me. My chest constricts. Something happened.

"Where is Harley?" I demand, looking around frantically.

Viper turns on his stool and looks at me with regret swimming in the depth of his eyes.

"I don't know, man. We got here, and next thing I know, I'm waking up on the fucking ground?" His statement more of a question than an answer.

I look to Grudge for more of an explanation.

"She did this. She ran off again," he explains.

"Did what? Hurt Viper?" I shake my head in disbelief. She wouldn't hurt Viper, no matter who she thinks she is, she would never hurt any one of our members.

"Yes. I told you... She's sick, son."

"No, she wouldn't leave." I shake my head and look at the door. Not again, she wouldn't leave without me.

"She did, she's not well and you know it. The sooner you fucking respect that, the sooner we can get back to club business. Where our focus needs to be." His words grate on my last nerve.

He reaches over the bar and grabs a plastic bag filled with buds of weed and tosses it at me. I catch it, a puzzled expression on my face.

"What the fuck is this?"

He looks at me like I should know what this is about. "We need better shit." He looks to Viper, who looks to the floor. His hand drops holding the icepack.

I cannot believe Grudge is wanting to discuss this now when Harley is out there somewhere.

I throw the bag of hash back at him.

"Maybe if you used Bud as our farmer, you wouldn't have such shit crop," I growl. It's the same thing I've been telling him. Even I don't smoke the club's shit and I can get it for free.

"I told everyone you turned against your kind if this isn't proof enough—"

I stomp forward and Viper stands in between us.

"Easy," he mutters.

"Why, because I care about Harley?" My chest pressed against Viper's hand, I raise my head slowly and glare at Grudge. "If I find out you did something to her... I will kill you," I threaten. The entire clubhouse goes silent as I just threatened my president. My teeth grind, my jaw tight as I stare at his soulless green eyes.

"Dude," Viper scorns me. But I don't back down, I know who the real untrustworthy person is in this room, and it's Grudge.

"You think I did something to my own blood?" Grudge scoffs, a stupid fucking look crossing his face.

I know he did something to her, and when I find her... I will be back and taking that fucking gavel.

Turning, I slam the doors to the club open and stomp outside.

The air is so hot and thick I feel like I'm not even breathing. Without Harley, I'm not.

"Where are you going?" Viper hollers.

"To find my ol' lady."

"I'm coming," he hurries up behind me.

"No, if you do, Grudge will out you," I try and protect him.

He looks away, blood staining his forehead.

"Man, Harley is like a sister to me. I'm coming with." He hits me with serious eyes. Bud steps up behind him. His hat lowered, but stance telling me he's breaking his loyalty to the club too.

"Let's do it then." I jerk the car door open.

22

HARLEY

L ittle black beads swarm in my eyes, my head heavy and mouth dry. Blinking a few times, a ceiling comes into view. I'm cold and uncomfortable. I'm definitely not at the club.

Sitting up, I notice I'm not moving. Whimpering, I look down and notice my arms belted to a hard bed, my legs and ankles the same way. Where- where am I?

I look around finding an empty room, the smell of lemon and urine strong. Panic begins to sink into my stomach. I jerk my arms, but they don't move. Becoming hysterical, I twist my body and kick my legs trying to free myself from the hard bed. The belts around my wrist and ankles are so tight my toes and fingers begin to tingle.

"Hello!" my voice echoes in the empty room. "BENJI!" I scream. "Benji, help!" I cry, staring at the harsh lights from above. They're so bright my eyes water. Even when I close them you can see them.

"All right little missy, that'll be enough." A raspy voice informs. My head whips to the side and I see an older lady in a white nurse gown and a white cap on her gray hair. She looks like she stepped out of a seventies horror movie.

"Who are you? Where am I?" I ask frantically. My mouth dry from breathing and screaming, my tongue sticks to the roof of my mouth.

"You're right where you need to be," she tells me with a tight-lipped smile. She doesn't make eye contact as she grabs something off a metal tray in the corner, her back facing me. I try and lift my head to see what she's doing but I'm restrained and can't lift far off the bed.

"Can you call my dad, he's the president of the Shadow Keepers MC. He will get me out of ..." I look around. "Whatever this is."

She turns, a needle in her hand. Her gray eyes and pale skin making her look ghostly.

"Aw yes, the old biker routine." Her cold blue eyes find mine and a chill strikes me right in the chest.

"Wh-what?" I look at her confused.

"Harley, there is no club and there's no Benji. I really hoped having you sedated so long you would let that story go."

"What are you talking about?" I snap, my confusion turning to anger.

She sighs, tilting her head to the side. "Your parents are a part of the Catholic community, and you're very sick with Dissociative Identity Disorder. That's why you're in here, so God can save you." She smiles, but I'm not smiling.

"No, that's not true. Benji is real, my club is real!" I stress. "Where am I? Tell me where I am!" I demand.

She rolls her eyes as if I'm crazy and steps over to me. The smell of cigarettes strong, and I notice her fingers are tinged yellow. Her cold hands press against my bare thigh, and I try and jerk away from her. Her clinical touch seeping into my skin and freezing my veins. But it's no use with these belts holding me in place, I'm at her mercy.

"You're in a hospital. And Benji is someone you made up in your head. A dream from the sedatives possibly. However, If you keep this up I'll have to be the bad guy and will have you moved back to the west wing."

Snarling, I glare at her. "Hospital? West wing?" My face contorts into anguish.

"My life isn't a dream!" My voice so loud it cracks.

"You've never made anything up before, thinking it was real?" She shoots me a cold look that has me holding my breath.

The way she's so serious, I'm starting to second guess myself. Is the Shadow Keepers something I made up? It's possible with my condition. I shake my head. No, it's real. I feel Benji in my heart and soul, and can still hear his voice in my head. I look down at my thumb where I wore Benji's ring, and it's bare.

My bottom lip trembles as the coldest chill I've ever felt strikes me in the chest.

"Please, hold still," she warns.

"Fuck you!" I jerk away from her. "SOMEONE HELP!" I scream, tears filling my eyes.

"You asked for it," she hisses and drives the needle right into my thigh. I swear it hits bone it hurts so bad. Burning, stinging, mind-numbing coldness shoots into my veins.

My entire body instantly goes weak, my vision blurring.

"No, stop! Please!" I pathetically beg. "You don't... you understand..." I begin to lose track of what I was saying. Fuzzy warm feelings buzzing through me.

"There is no club, Harley. There is no Benji, either," she repeats, her voice echoing like an old bell. "Repeat after me," she prompts.

My head rolls to the side, drool sliding out of the corner of my mouth. How'd that get there? My mouth was so dry seconds ago.

Voices in my head scream for help, but nothing comes out as I lay in a pool of sedatives.

"No, it's real," I sob, my throat clogging with emotion and

numbness. Tears slip from my eyes and roll down my motionless face.

"It's not," she whispers into my ear. Her rancid breath the last thing I breathe in as everything goes... black.

———

"ARE YOU WITH US, HARLEY?" A male voice echoes in my throbbing head. My eyes flutter open and the image of a man in a white lab coat doubles. I blink a few times, trying to get the image to stay still.

I was hoping being here was a nightmare and I would wake up in the club but the smell of lemon and piss tells me I'm still in hell.

"You're in the Arizona Psychiatric Hospital. You don't remember being a patient here?"

My eyes roll and I try to sit up, my back and sides very sore. My arms are suddenly jerked into place and I notice off-white belts restraining me to a bed. That's right, I'm tied to a bed. My eyes snap from the belts to the man standing before me.

"You were very hostile and we wanted to make sure you as well as our staff were safe," he informs. Now that I'm fully awake I can see him better. He looks to be in his thirties, blond hair with darker highlights, and no muscle tone to his body of what I can see. The way his nose points up at the end and his eyes narrow in on me. I can tell he thinks he's better than me. He's in control and he loves it.

"Where is Benji?" I demand.

The man clears his throat, frustration wrinkling his forehead.

"Harley," he leans forward on his knees, "there is no Benji, there is no club. We've been through this. It's all made up in your head, and you if you keep talking like this, you'll never get out of here. Do you understand?"

"Who are you?" My voice breathy.

"I come in once a week to check on my patients. I was told you were having a rough day, so I came to check on you. I'm Dr. Witterchecker."

My chest strikes with anger, my eyes as wide as saucers. He's lying. He's a fucking liar! Sobbing, I look down, my eyes falling on my tree line tattoo on my arm, and the saying, "Learn to get lost a little bit," striking me in the chest like a thunderbolt.

My eyes widen, my heart fluttering with hope that my being here is temporary.

"Then explain this," I ask through gritted teeth. The belts jingle as I tug my tattooed arm in his direction.

The man looks down at my tattoo, his thick caterpillar brows inching inward.

"You like to travel. It's in your file. I assume you thought desecrating your body would make you feel more adventurous." He shrugs, folding his hands in his lap.

My jaw drops, that little bit of hope I had in my chest snuffed out. Adventurous, that sounds like a load of crap.

"Who is paying you?" I growl.

"Maybe coming into population was too soon," he murmurs to himself. He's making me feel crazy, I'm not crazy!

"Fuck you! Fuck you! Fuck you!" I try and lunge at him, but am whipped back.

I scream, jerking the restraints so hard my right wrist snaps.

"Nurse!" Dr. Witterchecker moves to the side so the scary nurse can come in the room. She goes to the metal table and I continue freeing myself. My wrist burns, and aches from breaking it, but I push through the pain.

"I'm not crazy. I'll kill you. I'll kill you all!" I scream hysterically. Cold hands press into my thigh and the sting of the needle drowns me into the deep dark as I'm sedated again.

"Harley, come out from under the bed and meet Mr. Burt."

Squeezing my mermaid doll to my chest I peer out from under the bed and see a man in black underwear. He's old and wrinkly looking and has his hands on his hips. He looks mean and unfriendly.

"Do you want to come say hi?" Mom asks nicely. I look at the man again, and he smiles while nodding his head. A little voice in my head telling me to hide further in the darkness the bed held for me.

I shuffle under the bed to get away from them both. "No," I scream. The last time I came out for one of Mommy's friends, he made me uncomfortable. He kept petting me, and ...

"Come out and say hi!" Mother snaps, her fake friendly tone now gone. Bending down she grabs one of my legs from under the bed, a lit cigarette hanging from her mouth as she attempts to force me out of hiding. My nails dug into the floor as I scream for the bugs in the wall to help me. My eyes filling with so many tears I couldn't see in front of me anymore.

"Mommy, please no!" I begin to kick and squirm back under the bed.

The man crouches down and tries grabbing at my arms. Looking over my shoulder I use my free leg and I kick him in the face.

"MOTHER—" the man snaps upright holding his face.

"Oh my God, I'm so sorry!" Mother rushes to his side, not caring about me. She's worried I might have hurt him and has her back to me. Slipping out from the under my bed, I run to my bedroom window and quickly I open it, and fall out. The sting in my ankle not slowing me down, I run.

Bare feet sticking to the ground, legs cold from the night, I run until I see black.

23

TWO DAYS LATER

HARLEY

Staring out the window of my room, I run my finger along the condensation forming on the window. There's grass and benches in the backyard of the hospital. Patients who are stoned out of their mind wandering around mindlessly, they look like zombies. Their hair looks like it hasn't been brushed in days, and their gowns flow in the wind showing off pale bare asses of every shape and size. I wonder if I will be like them one day. Lost to the world and high on my daydreams. I was released from my bed yesterday, and my legs feel like twigs from not using them. My kneecaps feeling like they may succumb to my weight at any moment, and my arm is casted in blue due to the broken wrist I got in during my fit of rage the other day. I've never had a broken limb before.

If I were at the club, I'd have all the brothers sign it.

My fingers dip and curve against the cool glass until I spell out the name Benji. I've had no blackouts the last two days due to all the sedation. Farrah has gone to hide. I frown at that thought. I wonder if she's gone for good. I don't know what life is like not having her around, it scares me yet excites me.

I still don't know what is real and what isn't. I keep hoping every time I defy the staff their sedation will bring me back to Benji and the club *if*, in fact, they are a dream. The only thing I've seen though is things as a little girl. Living in that trailer with my mom and things I never wanted to remember. They've surfaced and it makes me feel like a different person replaying them. I was strong growing up, but only because Farrah made me strong. When I couldn't handle something, Farrah took over. It was easy to hide behind her, now that she might be gone though... there's no hiding. It's just cold hard life.

Turning, I slide down against the cold brick making up the walls of my room, my ass coming to the concrete floor. I wince, my thigh aching from all the needle jabs.

I run my damp finger over the tree line tattoo on my arm and the saying underneath it, "Learn to get lost a little bit."

"Baby," I whisper to myself. This was not done because I like to fucking adventure, or go hiking. They're all fucking lying here. They have to be, and if they're not... I don't care. Benji and the club are a lie I will live in for the rest of my life. It's where I want to be.

———

SITTING in a circle with three other patients, I bite at my nails nervously. They've grown out the few days I've been here. Must be the horse vitamins they keep forcing down my throat every morning. The white gown I'm wearing does nothing to hide my pebbled nipples from the chilly air and I have to cross my arms to conceal them from the male patients. I swear they keep it below freezing in here on purpose.

I've seen two of the three patients sitting in the circle before. One is Jessilynn. She has long blonde hair and often braids it when she's nervous. I can't figure out why she's in here though, she seems normal enough. The other is Memphis, half of her head is burned, leaving charred hair straight across her scalp.

She has the darkest saddest eyes I've ever seen, and burn marks all over her arms and face. I overheard a nurse saying she burned herself because of the voices in her head. She scares me.

"Jacob, why don't we start with you today," Nurse Jackie looks to the third patient. She's the horror story nurse I can't stand. Always smelling of cigarettes and vodka.

I haven't met Jacob yet. He's tall, slender, and pale as hell. He has a blue cast on his right arm that looks just like mine, and he looks sad. Like everyone else in here.

"What the fuck do you want me to say exactly?" he clips, his eyes contouring into anger. He's very resentful, and the way he's breathing I can tell he's about to explode.

"Why don't you start with why you're in here." Nurse Jackie smiles, oblivious to this grenade about to blow.

He looks up under his lashes at everyone as if he's embarrassed of why he is in here and I quickly look away. I don't have it in me to find him. I'm already fighting myself.

"I tried to run my Jeep into a tree," he shrugs, pulling at the strings of his gown. "I can't even kill myself right," he mutters.

"Why is death an option for you?" she prods, and my mouth drops at her insensitivity. How can she be so cold and forthcoming about something so serious? She doesn't care about anyone in here. We are all hazard pay to her.

Jacob stands abruptly, knocking over the plastic chair.

"I'm fucking done with this shit." He throws his hands out in distress, his face red. Jessilynn braids her hair not caring to the commotion, and Memphis cries hysterically at the chaos, holding her blanket close to her chest like a small child would.

I just watch.

Jackie sighs and looks at me as it's my turn to open up to the group of strangers. My spine stiffens and I look to the tree line on my arm. I don't want to talk to her. She makes me feel uncomfortable with her hollow stare, the smile constantly plastered on her face tells me she likes our pain. One snap of her fingers and two men will stride in here and stab me in the leg with whatever is in that syringe and put me in a mind-numbing state. Nightmares and reality of my mother swimming in my head for countless hours.

"Harley?" I jeer at the sound of my name. The way my name falls from her tongue is eerie.

Like Jacob, I stand and excuse myself to my room. I need some space. Everything here is so confusing and crazy. Having people in your face the whole time is too much.

"Harley, you cannot leave!" Jackie tries to grab at me as I walk by. I look over my shoulder with a glare and pick up my pace.

Before I know what's happening, my feet are lifted from the stained floor by two large hands on each of my arms.

"Get off me!" I don't know who has a hold of me, but I can tell it's someone I don't want touching me. Their hands are large and biting into the fat of my arms, the little effort they have in lifting me telling me they're bigger than I am. Looking over my left shoulder, I find an orderly who is directed to manhandle the patients when disobeying. I've seen him do it a few times the last couple of days.

"You want to go to your room so bad? You got it," he growls with a low tone. I find his name tag. "Peg?"

He smiles like a scumbag and I notice his two front teeth are gold. He reminds me of the men in my dreams with my mother and I go limp in his arms. He tries to place me on my feet, and I begin to kick and punch at him to let me go.

"Get off me, you troll looking fucker!" My pain and hollers echo through the halls, but nobody even glances in my direction. The sound of agony is habitual here. A lullaby to every patient's path to their routine nightmare. Without it, they wouldn't be able to function.

My feet shuffle and slam against the ground as he drags me to my room. My broken wrist protests and aches as I try and resist. Entering my room, he tosses me on the hard bed like a throw blanket, and Nurse Jackie is suddenly right beside me restraining my arms and ankles with the belts on the side of my bed.

I struggle by yanking my wrist and trying to twist free. The cast begins to shred around my arm, little frays of blue fluttering in the air. My eyes burn with the urge to cry, but I breathe through it as I scream like a mad woman.

She turns, allowing Peg to finish tying my feet to the bed.

"Let me go! I don't belong here!"

The unmistakable stab in my thigh has me whimper as everything becomes dizzy. I relax into the stiff bed, my jaw becoming lax.

"*Harley? Harley, where are you?*" My mother's eerie voice sounds in my head.

"Benji," I whisper, willing him to be true and come rescue me.

"There you go," Nurse Jackie coos, fingers in my hair feeling like snakes. I drift to a world of nightmares.

I hope I see Benji there.

24

HARLEY

"You new?"

Opening my eyes to the unfamiliar voice, everything is blurry at first. I feel sick to my stomach and my head throbs.

"If you don't eat, those sedatives can make you puke," the voice comes again.

Raising my head, I rub at my temples trying to ease the ache.

Wait, my hand is free. I look down, noticing I'm not restrained. Why would they release me so quickly?

"Fuckers are restraining happy around here." I finally turn toward the female voice, finding Jessilynn sitting in the window seat of my room. Her legs are pressed to her chest, and a lit cigarette dangles between two of her fingers as she stares out the dirty glass. The little bit of sun that shines through casts a glow against her skin. She has the saddest blue eyes I've ever seen. They look like the depths of the ocean nobody can explore, for they'd never be able to reach the top again if they tried.

Her face is pale, a few freckles painting the bridge of her nose and her lips are so pink you'd think she has lipstick on but that's not allowed in here. It brings life to her face that you can't look away from.

She reminds me of one of those glass dolls you see people put on their shelves.

"What are you doing in here?" I ask with a scratchy voice. Every word I speak echoes in my head from the sedative I was injected with. My leg sore, stiff, and bruised from all the needles being jabbed into it.

"You new here?" She gazes at me, tilting her head to the side in question.

"I don't know... am I?" I ask, not sure if I'm new and the nurses are lying about my life just being a dream... or if they're telling the truth and everything I thought my life was is a facade.

She shrugs, looking back out the grimy window. Her gown is three sizes too big and falls off her shoulder as she situates herself in the window.

"I've never seen you before, but that doesn't mean you haven't been here awhile. The facility has another wing for the really fucked up people. They're sedated most of the time I hear, and we don't see them," she looks at me with sad eyes. "Did you come from there?"

Sitting up, I sigh. "I don't know, maybe." I look to my hospital gown. If I was sedated the whole time I was over there, how would I know?

"So it is true. You're the Forgotten Girl?" her statement more of a question.

"Forgotten Girl?"

"Yeah," she holds her hand out with the cigarette, her brows furrowing in. "Like, you forget who you are, and where you've been." She tilts her head to the side, placing the cigarette between her pink lips. "Or maybe someone forgot you?"

I tear my eyes from hers and look down at my feet, fighting off the feelings of emptiness and loneliness. Most likely from being the forgotten girl, everyone seems to know about except the girl herself. Me.

Hell, even I've forgotten myself. Who am I? Where did I come from? Is there anyone on the outside for me?

"I heard one of the nurses talking about you having a split personality or some shit."

"I don't know how long I've been here, but one thing is for sure... nobody is coming for me," I whisper. I'm starting to think Benji isn't real because the Benji I know... would be here by now.

"Well, Forgotten Girl. It's movie night, get your ass up and let's go see what they chose for us."

"Movie night?"

"Yeah, once a week they put a shitty movie on in the caged TV. If King Kong gets lucky and Nurse Jackie lets him fuck her in the office, sometimes we can switch it to cable and watch The Kardashians." She waggles her brows. "It's the most excitement we get around here."

"King Kong?" I don't remember anyone working here by that name.

"Troll looking fucker?" She tilts her head to the side, repeating what I called the orderly when he was dragging me to my room.

"Oh," I laugh.

Climbing out of the window, paint chips flicker to the ground around her bare feet.

Grabbing my hand, I feel every bone in her hand, it's cold too, as she ushers me off the bed. Sliding off the mattress on wobbly feet, I follow her into the main room. I'm cold and hurt everywhere. I cross my arms feeling vulnerable, and anxious. There are four tables placed about the main room, words of anger and pain scratched into the tops, and the metal chairs rusted and uncomfortable looking surrounding them.

"Jessilynn, we've told you about freeing the patients," Nurse Jackie schools as she walks into the room holding a DVD. Jackie glares at me and I quickly look away. I don't want to be tied down anymore.

It's crazy how fast they beat down your self-confidence here.

"Oops." Jessilynn rolls her eyes, plopping into a random seat. She pats the chair next to her, indicating she wants me to sit next to her. Carefully I sit by her, the cold metal reaching through my gown and freezing my ass. I cross my legs and sit beside her as the rest of the patients wander in.

Nurse Jackie pulls keys from her white jacket unlocking the cage surrounding the TV and DVD player on the wall. She inserts the movie and slams it closed. Locking it, her eyes giving a once over of the group menacingly.

"Any problems and the movie is off." She raises a brow before heading into the office behind us, King Kong following her. The door clicks shut and the blinds are pulled down.

I look to Jessilynn who smiles in knowing. It's the first time I've seen her look happy since I've been here.

ET starts to play on the little screen and it takes me aback.

"ET?" I question, surprised by the old movie.

"Yup, it's one of her favorites, probably because she looks like the creepy fucking alien," Jessilynn states seriously. Looking closer, Nurse Jackie does kind of look like ET. I snicker.

Ten minutes into the movie, I grow bored. I glance over my shoulder to the office and find that the blinds are not pulled down all the way. Bending down, I peek under the blinds and see thick hairy legs thrusting in between the milky thick thighs of Nurse Jackie. The desk rocking, and tapping against the stone wall.

Jessilynn nudges me. "Told ya."

I cringe, it's pretty gross looking. Images in my sedative state will never erase what I just saw.

Jessilynn stands from her chair and climbs on top of the table before walking across the other three like they're lily pads.

"What are you doing?" I ask nervously. I look to the office behind us, but Nurse Jackie and Peg are lost in their own world to see what Jessilynn is doing. Reaching the caged TV, she fingers out a pencil sitting next to it and uses the eraser to press buttons on the side of the TV. The Kardashians suddenly appear on the screen.

She bows as everyone sits up in their seat, the entire group coming to life. Memphis smiles a crooked grin and claps in excitement. Her burnt blanket hanging off her lap.

I can't tell if Jessilynn is really crazy or stupid brave. I like her.

Jessilynn walks back across the tables and sits next to me, the smell of sweet lemons surrounding me. Her tongue slides back and forth along her bottom lip in a mischievous way, and I shake my head with a smile. However, on the inside I break for her. How long has she been locked up in here? Does she have family? Why is she even here?

THE OFFICE DOOR suddenly opens and Nurse Jackie scowls with just fucked me hair. Her uniform buttoned up wrong and her hat is missing. Her eyes whip to the TV and her mouth drops.

"WHO DID THIS!" She looks to the group. "Who changed the movie?"

Everyone goes stiff, and Jessilynn rolls her eyes. She's not scared of Jackie and I find that admirable.

"Everyone to their room! Sedatives for everyone!"

"Chill your fucking tits, will ya. I did it. You have shitty taste in movies, Jackie!" Jessilynn admits, kicking her legs up on the table.

Black beady eyes fall to Jessilynn and goosebumps rise along my skin.

"Well then everyone has *you* to thank for their good night

sleep then," Jackie replies in a bitch tone. Even though Jessilynn confessed, we're all still getting stuck with needles and toxins.

I stand, not okay with this.

"You can't just put us out for a nap whenever you feel like it!" I defend, this can't be legal. Who is running this place?

"I can, and you'll be the first. Keep it up and you'll go in the hole with Franky!"

"Franky?" I look to Jessilynn. Is that another patient or something?

"Lobotomy," Jessilynn replies, and her eyes show fear for the very first time. My mouth drops, my heart skipping a beat. No, this can't be okay. This can't be real!

Jackie snaps her fingers and Peg marches toward me.

He fists me by the casted arm and I whimper in pain.

"Ow, let go!" I try and tug away from him, but my arm can't take any more abuse.

"Get off her!" Jessilynn jumps on him, pounding on his back with a solid fist. She's so small compared to him it makes me scared for her. I can't let her get hurt defending me.

I scream, pulling my feet off the ground to make it harder for him to control me. I kick, slap, and even try to bite him. The rest of the group screams, cries, and some even clap that we're standing up to the staff. The chaos rings in my ears and pumps adrenaline through my limbs.

"I want to talk to who is in charge!" I demand. "You can't treat us like animals!"

Just when I think Jessilynn and I are gaining control, a jab in my leg warns me I'm about to fall into dreamland, and that whoever is in charge, I'm not. I fall to the floor in a paralyzed state, my head thrashing against the grimy ground.

Jessilynn slams to the ground next to me. Her fall so great, her eyebrow begins to bleed into her eye.

"See you on the other side, Forgotten Girl," she slurs as she was sedated just like me. We stare at each other for a lost moment before we both escape the horror of our prison.

Benji

ME, Viper, and Bud riding in my El Camino we drive to June's house. We've been to the shelters, the hotels in the area, and even the emergency rooms. I can't find any trace of where Harley is.

The last person that saw her, was June. So, I'm going to find that bitch if I have to chase her across the state. June escaped though, and I know Grudge let her go. She knows what happened to Viper and Harley and I will strangle the fucking truth from her if I have to. I need to find Harley, and every day I don't... it's a punch in the gut that I let the one girl I love... get away.

"What makes you think this bitch is dumb enough to run back home?" Viper asks, his feet hanging out my car's window.

"I don't know that she's there for sure, but if she's not then we'll figure something else out."

Heading back to June's house it looks empty. As if she moved in the last few days. Probably couldn't stand to see the sight of blood on her perfect floor. Images of her husband and a shoe sticking out of his skull too much for her.

"Fuck," I mumble under my breath.

"Let's try the school," Viper suggests. Inhaling a breath, and out of options, I head to the campus.

Pulling up to the main office I park and we all get out. College kids stare at us, parting like the Red Sea to let us walk through without skipping a step.

Going inside the main office there's a punk behind the front desk wearing a beanie. He looks stoned out of his mind and is flirting with a young girl in glasses.

Viper gets in line and I give him a look.

"What?" He looks at me with a confused grin.

"We don't wait in fucking line," I tell him softly. We're fucking big ass bikers. We don't do the right thing, what the fuck?

He rolls his eyes and pushes past the geeky girl.

"Is June here?" he asks, slamming his fists on the counter. Much better.

"Whoa, you're big!" The boy chuckles, looking Viper up and down. Leaning over the counter, I knock his stapler off the ledge. His eyes tear from Viper to me. "That's not really cool, man." His dopey tone draws out.

Bud steps around the corner and rips the phone from the wall, and this makes Dopey jump to attention.

"Uh, today is her last day, she was in her office last I heard!" He steps back, his body flush with the dirty glass behind him.

"Where is her office?" I ask.

He grabs a piece of paper off the corner of his desk and tosses it at me. I grab it before it flutters to the floor. It's a map of the campus, and it has June's office marked with a little star.

"Thanks." Viper gives him a curt nod. I swear he's the most polite outlaw I know.

Following the guide, we walk across the grass to a tall building. Going inside, it's dark and quiet. The only sound is our breathing and boots on the clean floor. Winding down a hallway, we find her in her office placing books into a brown cardboard box.

"Leaving so soon?" My tone grave. She whirls around in a gasp of surprise. She looks a fucking mess, much like the way I left her. Her hair is frizzy, her shirt untucked from her pencil skirt, and she has no makeup on.

She grabs a letter opener and points it at me in defense.

"Don't come any closer!"

Rubbing my chin, I laugh at her weak attempt to defend herself. Step by step, I get closer, and she does nothing. She doesn't have it in her to do anything.

"Where did they take my girl?" My eyes feast upon her, silently telling her not to fuck with me or that cheap piece of shit weapon she has will be in her throat.

Her eyes flick to Viper and Bud behind me.

"What happened to me?" Viper points to his head. I'm sure his confidence took a hit being knocked out like that.

"If I tell you—"

"I promise to leave you alone and never bother you again," I answer the ultimatum she's about to suggest, a smile wolfishly pulling at my lips.

"Ha, and I should just believe you?" Her face scrunches with distaste.

I press my palm to my chest.

"Scouts honor," Sarcasm dripping from my voice.

"You don't have a choice," Viper clips, slamming the door behind him. Her eyes widen, and the lump in her throat bobs as she swallows.

"I uh, the big guy." She holds her hand above her head to indicate his height.

"Grudge?" I prompt.

"Sure, he hit you with a tool or something." She looks to Viper.

"You sure?" I tilt my head to the side, and she silently nods. I look to Viper, and he turns, his shoulders rising and falling with anger. His hands rest on the bookcase, his fingers curl around the shelf.

He needs a second.

"And the girl?" I look back to June.

"You mean that crazy bitch?"

I grab her by the throat, my rings shining from the sunlight coming through the blinds.

"Easy now, that's my girl you're talking about," I inform gravely. Her sudden cocky attitude fades as fear swims in her eyes.

"I don't know." She begins to cry, and it does nothing for me. Her tears are a waste of emotion, as I'm this close to strangling her.

"Try," I seethe.

"Some guys in white coats drugged her, put her in this, um, this straight jacket of sorts." She begins to tremble in my hold, and it makes me want to hurt her more. She's so vulnerable, I can't help but want to choke her.

"Grudge had her put away," Bud says softly, nearly a whisper behind me. I look over my shoulder at him, his hat pulled down and arms crossed. The fucking mute talks.

Viper loses it and throws the entire bookcase to the ground. Little polite outlaw turned fucking Hulk.

I loosen my grip on June and slip a piece of her hair behind her ear.

"See, that wasn't so hard," I rasp softly.

She nods, tears streaming down her face.

"You know not to speak a word of me, my boys, or Harley to anyone?" I tilt my head to the side, her pathetic sobbing even worse from this angle.

"I won't say anything. I'm going to live with my dad and help him on his tour. I swear!"

"I'm not worried, because if I hear otherwise... there's more of us," I nod my head toward Viper and Bud.

"Okay, yes," she cries. Her cheeks red and swollen from the tears.

"Your daddy, better never come near my club again, he fucked his connection with us. Understand?"

"Yes. I promise, you will never see us again," she blubbers.

"Let's go, boys," I rasp, and leave June to run to Daddy.

Climbing back into my car, Viper holds his phone up showing me a map.

"There are two state hospitals for the mentally ill in the state, and my money is on this one." He points to red tag on the far side of Arizona.

"Why?" I furrow my brows.

"It's funded by the state, which Governor Timothy has donated generous amounts to." His left brow raises in telling.

"Motherfucker." I grip the wheel tight, my foot heavy on the accelerator. Grudge really did have Harley locked away. He turned his back on his own flesh and blood. Harley being locked away protects him from everything she knows about him, and I think Harley knows more than she even knows.

"So, what's the plan?" Viper asks, running his hand through his blondish hair.

"We get my girl." I flick my gaze to him. "End of."

25

BENJI

Pulling up to the front of the haunted-looking hospital, I walk around the back and pop the trunk. I grab a rifle, machete, and .45 as Viper helps himself to a load of weapons himself. We're quiet, not speaking a word as we reflect on what's about to happen. More than likely, someone will try and play the hero, someone will cry, but there's always that one person that gives us what we want. We need to find that person to get to Harley. Sooner rather than later.

Jogging up the cracked steps of the hospital, the dead bushes on each side sways from the dry wind. Bud tries the door, but it's locked. I look at him with a puzzled look.

"Do you have a gun?"

He doesn't answer me.

"Should we press the buzzer?" Viper asks, pointing to the speaker on the left wall.

Lifting my .45, I fire a bullet into the lock, and tug the door open.

"Or not," Viper mutters, following me inside.

The tiled floor is an off-white color, the smell of piss and shit strong. You can hear screaming echoing down the hall, and the lights flickering from above give this place the perfect haunted feel.

"This is fucking scary right off the bat," Viper whispers.

"Just stay close," I tell him. I look around, following the hall until we reach a cage gate.

I shoot the lock and the door opens. Two men with robes wonder around, oblivious to us marching in here with guns. They look like zombies. They're so fucked up on medicine they don't even know where they are.

"Jesus Christ!" Viper rasps, he steps up to the bald one, his balls hanging out of his boxers. Viper snaps his fingers in front of the guys face, but he doesn't even blink. It's as if he's gone; autopilot.

I look to the next gate down the hall, my insides coiling with adrenaline. I'm scared to see what state Harley is in.

"Let's find Harley." I shake my head.

Viper reaches the next gate and shoots it open. Patients on the other side scream, and a huge man wearing a white shirt and black jeans steps in front of us.

He tries to grab at me, and I raise my gun to his head. His beady eyes squint, and I can tell we're going to have a hero on our hands.

"Step aside," I warn. He laughs and lunges at me again. I fire a bullet right into his skull and he drops to my feet.

An older woman steps out of a secured office, a white cap on her head. She's a nurse and looks evil as shit.

"Where's Harley?" I ask, scratching the back of my neck with my warm bloody barrel.

"SECURITY!" She slams a red button on the wall and lights begin to flash on the ceiling.

"Now why'd you do that?" I look at her irritated.

"Fuck, we need to hurry, man," Viper seems alarmed.

"Start checking rooms," I order, and Bud opens the closest door to him.

I open a door and find a half-burnt chick rocking back and forth on her bed. I close the door, not wanting to disturb her.

Heading to the next door, the nurse runs toward Bud with a syringe in her hand.

I slip the rifle off my shoulder, and fire bullets into her stomach. Her body flies into a brick wall from the force. Blood spraying the floor and tables.

Bud looks at the body, his hat pulled so low I can't see if he's grateful I just saved his ass or not.

"I—I know Harley."

I turn, a small nurse shaking in her white sneakers.

"Where is she?" I narrow my eyes and point the rifle at her.

"This way." She points down the long hallway.

"Thank you." My eyes earnest, I tell her how appreciative I am with my tone.

Harley

Commotion stirs me from the depths of a blurry darkness. My head throbs, my thigh bruised and stiff from all the shots. My stomach coils into a tight knot making me nauseous. I try to move my head to the side so if I puke I won't drown in it. Though, I don't even remember the last time I ate.

"Where is she?"

I blink rapidly. I know that voice. Is it a dream or reality though? Using my elbows, I try and push myself up, but I'm restrained to the bed.

Stomping echoes through the hallway right outside my room, and I stress my eyes to look down as far as I can.

A small shaking nurse stops in my doorway, she administers our daily medication. Her makeup is smeared as she cries from a gun barrel pressed to her temple. I run my eyes up the weapon to familiar tattooed arms before finally meeting angry hostile blue eyes.

"Benji?" I croak. He steps to my bedside, looming over me. The smell of leather and weed bringing me back to everything I was questioning was real. "You're not a dream," I weep. I try and move my arm needing to touch him, I want to feel him and see that he is real.

He chuckles.

"I wouldn't say I would be one to appear in dreams, but by the looks of this place I guess you could think that."

He palms my face and tears fill my eyes. His hand is warm, the small pound of his heart in his veins telling me he is real.

"I'm here now, Harley," his voice raspy.

Biting my bottom lip, I nod.

He's real. I'm not crazy.

I'm getting out of here.

Benji

LOOKING down at Harley I barely recognize her. She's lost weight and is frail. Her ocean colored eyes seem dull, like they haven't seen sun in days. Seeing her restrained to this bed has me ready to kill every person working here.

"I'm here, and I'm getting you out," I explain with a shaky voice. I wasn't sure I found the right place when we got here, in a way I was hoping I didn't when I pulled up to this hell hole, but June was right, Harley is here. Grudge had her locked away, which means he knocked Viper out.

Quickly, I unbuckle the belts around her wrist and ankles. They're tight as hell leaving dark markings on her beautiful skin. I look up, noticing for the first time she has a blue cast on her arm. My jaw ticks as I run my fingers over the cast.

"What the fuck did they do to you?" I sigh. Seeing my club princess in such bad shape has me gritting my teeth until they nearly crack. Grudge will pay for this. I'll fucking kill him.

Looking over my shoulder Bud is standing guard by the door.

"Hold my rifle." I toss him my gun, and he catches it midair. With my hands now free, I scoop my arms under her and lift her. The hospital gown she's wearing shifts showing her bruised polka dotted thigh.

My chest constricts with a burning sensation as I take in the dark purple and yellow splotches marring her beautiful skin.

"Benji," she slurs.

"I'm not letting go." I put her arms around my neck, and turn toward the hallway Viper and Bud stand in with guns raised.

Boots stomping into the dirty floor, I head down the narrow exit. Lights flicker above and the flash from that bitch hitting the alarm.

"Let's go," I instruct the boys. Viper looks over his shoulder, his eyes widening at Harley's state.

"Jesus, is that her?"

My brows furrow with worry. "Yeah, let's get her home," I mutter.

"Wait!" A female voice has us stop and turn our heads.

A skinny blonde in a hospital gown stands on a table. She's pale with bright pink lips and doesn't seem afraid of us. Bud points the rifle at her, but she seems unfazed by it.

"Take me with you." She lifts her chin.

Viper laughs, and I shake my head. That ain't happening.

Harley tries to raise her head to look at the girl.

"Easy, baby," I warn her.

"Take. Her." Harley wheezes, her beautiful eyes flicking to mine. She must know this girl.

Leaning my head down, I run my nose up her cheek, the smell of her not recognizable. I don't smell her cheap bubblegum, the smell of leather and weed vacant. It kills me.

"Who knows why she's in here, we can't risk it," Bud states in a near whisper. This is the most I've heard him talk in one day, and it's fucking surprising.

"Come the fuck on." Viper waves her on, taking command.

I grit my teeth at him making the decision without me, but I got what I came for and shouldn't be taking on any more.

"She's your fucking problem," I inform him.

I step over the charge nurse I blew away with my rifle, and a bodyguard looking fucker that tried to play hero. Blood pools around their dead bodies as we exit caged door after caged door.

"Wait, my ring," Harley groans. I stop in my tracks, my eyes falling to her hand. My ring is missing. She looks up at me with desperate eyes, if the ocean could cry Harley's eyes would be the perfect example. We ain't leaving without that damn ring.

Turning where I stand, alarms blaring I head into the main office. If anyone has it, I bet it's in there. The nurse that helped us is hiding in the corner and shrieks when she sees me stomp inside.

"Where is her ring," I bark. Quickly she opens a cabinet and flips through some colored files.

"H-here," she displays a baggie with Harley's skull ring.

"Take it," I whisper. Harley reaches out and clutches the bag as if it contained her heart. My ring really means something to her.

I kiss her forehead, as her shaky hands slide the ring back on her thumb.

Finally making it to my El Camino, the blonde bitch and Viper crawl in , and I slip in next with Harley close to my chest. My fingers tangle in her hair, it's dry and matted. Her heartbeat slow against my chest, and it scares me to think what she went through in there.

"Where to?" Bud asks sliding in behind the steering wheel.

"Home," Harley moans, snuggling up to me.

God, it feels good to have her in my arms again. I was scared I'd never see her again. Though, I'd never give up looking for her until I did find her.

"What the fuck are we going to say to Grudge when we roll up to the clubhouse with his daughter in the car?" Viper scoffs. "He nearly killed me trying to hide her."

Harley's fingers pull into my cut hearing that her dad did this to her. She may be crazy, and may qualify to be in a mental institute, but when my feet are above ground and air in my lungs. She will never be in one of those places again.

"He's not going to be saying much." My tone cocky. "His mouth will be too full with the barrel of my gun shoved between his teeth."

26

BENJI

Pulling up to the clubhouse, the car is silent, the tension so thick you can bite it. Viper cocks his gun in the back seat, as does Bud. They know what's about to go down and have my back.

Once the club hears the transgressions of Grudge, they will all have my back. A new chain of command will reign over the club tonight.

Stopping in the middle of the courtyard, Harley slips off my lap and I open the door and step out. I look to the strange blonde bitch in the back seat and point at her.

"Keep Harley in this car." My tone not to be questioned. She nods with eyes the size of saucers.

I grab Harley by the chin, my touch soft and caring.

"Whatever happens here tonight, I want you to know I love you. If I die, you climb in that seat," I point to the driver seat, "and you run until you reach the border, do you understand?"

"Benji, you're scaring me. What are you going to do?" Her eyes look at me more innocent than ever. I hope she doesn't hate me when this is over.

"What I need to do to protect my girl and my club."

Taking a deep breath, I stand straight and pull my gun from my waistband. Twisting my neck back and forth, it cracks; loosening up for what's to come.

"You sure this is what you want to do, brother?" Viper gives me a concerned look.

"He turned his back on the brotherhood when he took our princess away. I'm taking the gavel, and nobody is standing in my way." I give him a pointed look.

"I got your back." His tone serious.

"Me too," Bud responds with a joint hanging out of his mouth, muffling his response.

We stomp toward the front doors of the club but before we can open them, Grudge and a few of his loyal goons stand behind him.

"Benji, where have you been?" he asks with a condescending tone. His arms stretched out wide. He's shirtless under his cut, and his jeans are unbuttoned. He looks like a slob, not a president or role model of our club

"Me?" I point my gun to my chest with a crooked smile. "Finding your daughter," I inform with a dead tone.

His face falls as his eyes sweep to my car. I step in front of it, blocking his view of Harley. He will never look at her again.

"You lied to us all," Viper chimes in. "What other lies do you have under that cut?"

I raise my gun, pointing it at Grudge. Bold green eyes stare into the barrel of my gun, his shoulders rising.

"What? You think you're going to kill me and take my club, son?" He laughs, the men behind him chuckling as well. They think it's a joke that I'm defending my colors.

"Oh yes, that is exactly what I plan to do." I tilt my head to the side. "You know why?"

"Entertain me," he grins.

"You locked our princess away, you killed Harley's mother, and you killed Buddy and Totty," I whisper that last part. The secret of Buddy and Totty that Harley and I had to live with for years is finally revealed. Everyone freezes, curious eyes looking at their president with disbelief.

"Is that true?" Viper looks at me with a blank stare.

"Don't listen to him." Grudge points to Viper.

Viper raises his gun, his face pale. "You knocked me out. You made it look like Harley did it, but you were the weak motherfucker that hit me from behind." Viper is very salty about being knocked out, as he should be. He looked up to Grudge like I did. He taught us a lot about being a man.

Hearing how he's turned his back on us all, it makes you question everything he's ever done.

"Son?" My dad's voice sounds behind Grudge, the crowd splitting to let my dad through. I inhale a shaky breath as my old man looks at me in distraught. "Wh-what are you doing?" He looks between me and Grudge. "Put down your weapons," Dad's voice shakes with age.

"Telling the truth, Dad."

"Your son called me a liar—" Grudge huffs, looking to my dad as if he should handle me. My dad and Grudge go way back, and it scares me whose side my father will take.

"You broke the creed of our brotherhood!" My rage rattles my voice.

"Is that true?" Dad looks to Grudge with old eyes.

"He killed my dad," Bud whispers, and everyone looks to him. The hat conceals his face lowered to where you can't see his eyes, but you can't miss the tear sliding down his smooth cheek.

"He had Harley locked away, told me she ran away again," I explain.

Dad's gray brows frown as he looks at Grudge with disrespect heavy in his tired eyes. It wasn't my intention to do this to my ol' man, to reveal the blood under the rug, but the club needs a man to step up, and I am.

"You turned your back on your own flesh and blood, how the fuck do you expect us to trust you?"

"Roadie... Who are you going to believe, eh? I mean—" Grudge tries to explain his actions but Dad raises his hand, cutting him off.

"You killed Buddy, and then had the nuts not to let his son take over his crops?" Dad asks with disbelief. It's no secret Bud has wanted to take over the growing of our weed business, he's good at what he does. But Grudge wouldn't have it for some reason. Now everyone knows why... too close to home after he killed Buddy. I rub the back of my head with my gun, the shit hitting the fan making me uncomfortable. Dad shakes his head at Grudge before slowly stepping away, tucking himself behind my back. It feels good to know Dad has my back. A couple of the men behind Grudge do the same as they take my side, leaving only two prospects behind Grudge. Two dumb ones.

The club is falling into my hands.

"Harley's sick, Benji!" Grudge tries to defend his actions of his daughter, but not of the patched-in brother he murdered.

"We're all a little twisted here, but we take care of our own," I recite our creed. Our new law.

That will be my first rule as president.

I raise my gun, my finger heavy on the trigger. Viper and Bud doing the same.

Grudge laughs silently, looking down as if he's about to do the right thing and handle this like we should. Burning out his colors on his back and kicking him out.

He looks up at me, green eyes fusing with mine own. His hand darting under his cut reaching for his gun in his leather holster. I grit my teeth, ignore the clutch in my chest as my .45 throws a bullet into his head. His skull cracking from the bullet sends chills up my spine and I breathe in the smell of his blood with the warm summer air. I just killed my president, a man I've looked up to like my own father since I was a kid.

I knew he wouldn't go about losing the gavel like a man is supposed to. A Shadow Keeper fights to the death.

Grudge falls to the ground, his eyes wide but lifeless. His head looking like someone dropped a watermelon on the ground. It's split, showing brain matter and veins.

Some club bitches scream, one dropping to her knees at the gruesome scene.

Viper and Bud fire their guns, taking out the two dipshit prospects behind him.

Stepping up to Grudge, I fire two more rounds into his chest just to make sure the Devil is dead. It hurts to see him like this, but it had to be done.

He broke our club, he took one of ours and locked them away, he killed our own and hid it. He couldn't be trusted anymore.

"DAD!" Harley screams, the pitter patter of her bare feet on the pavement. Looking up, I watch her as if she's in slow motion. Her hair blowing in the wind, tears down her cheeks, and her hospital gown flowing in the breeze.

I hold my right arm out and grab her before she makes contact with him. I fold her into my arms as she cries her pain into my chest. She falls to the ground and I go with her, holding her close

"It had to be done," I whisper into the top of her head. My own eyes stinging with the urge to cry. She loved the dad from when she was a little girl, not the dad that owned her as a woman.

"Daaaaad," she continues to cry, her body wracking within my own.

"Shhh, you're safe now, Harley." I coax her.

The blonde woman I told to watch Harley stands above us, her arms crossed and gown flapping around her legs. She looks over the bloody scene without blinking an eye. I wonder how fucking crazy she is?

"What's your name?" I ask her, rocking Harley back and forth to try and soothe her loss.

"Jessilynn," she replies with a sweet tone of voice.

"Well, Jessilynn you're ours now, you belong to the Shadow Keepers." She's seen too much to let her run with freedom.

"Viper, get her." He walks over to her, his boots sounding loud as he takes the crazy bitch away from the scene. I don't know who this chick is or where she comes from other than the asylum. Who knows if she will speak of what's happened here tonight. So, until we know more about her and if she can be trusted. She's going to have eyes on her ass all the time.

Harley twists in my lap, looking up at me with tear-filled eyes. She's so broken, but she's never looked more beautiful than she does right now. I look forward to putting her back together again, adding my pieces with hers.

Tucking my thumb under her chin I focus on her.

"He locked you away, lied to the club. He killed your mother, Harley. He went rogue and needed to be taken care of the Shadow Keepers' way. The memories you have of your dad are from when you were a kid, not the man that lays over there now."

Her tongue sweeps out, taking in a salty tear. Her head shaking back and forth as she looks away from the building.

"I knew he killed my mother, I just... I didn't want to believe it." Her words catch in her throat. I knew because I heard him talking about it with my dad when I was younger, but how does she know?

"How did you know?"

"I came too once and was sitting on a metal frame, with ash all around me. It took me a minute to figure out where I was, but it wasn't long before I realized... it was my old home. It had been burnt to the ground, and in my chest, I could feel that my father did it," she whispers.

"The Shadows have him now," I mutter. They will punish him

for his sins against the club and make him walk the path of hell. She looks up to me, a smirk pulling her dry lips into a smile.

"You think?"

"I know."

Some people believe in God, others don't. We believe our kind go to the land of bikers. Our god one that reigns the streets of outlaws, and takes them when it's their time.

Standing, I pull her to her feet and I look to the group.

"I am your president now, does anyone object to that?" I ask the crowd, knowing my ways of taking the gavel are not ethical. There should be a vote and probably a chapter meeting, but I have my way of doing things.

Everyone nods in agreement, and I pull Harley up close to my side.

"This is your club queen now and you will respect her as she stands behind me at every meeting. Rides with me on every run, and I will seek her advice on many club transactions. Is this a problem?"

I wait for someone to disagree as having a woman's view on club business is outlawed in our club.

"No," everyone answers, agreeing to let our princess in. Bud gives a curt nod, his arms crossed in front of his chest as he doesn't fucking speak.

"My first ruling as your president is Bud is now our grower."

Everyone looks to Bud and he looks around as if there might be another Bud amongst the group. I laugh.

Slowly, Bud grabs the bill of his hat and pulls it off. Gray wavy hair falls down his shoulders, and beautiful soulless eyes meet mine.

My eyes widen and everyone gasps.

He slides off his leather jacket and the gray Rolling Stones shirt from underneath show lines around his chest. Lines I've never seen until now. He lifts his shirt and a belly jewel dangles from his perfect navel. Duct tape wrapped around the breasts has me suck in a tight breath as he tears it off and a black sports bra is revealed to everyone.

Holy. Shit.

Harley giggles like she knew the whole time, and I'm floored. I'm speechless.

Bud is a chick. Walking around with a fucking pussy the whole time I thought he was a dude.

"About time," Bud smiles, tilting her head to the side. I snap my eyes to Harley. "You knew about this?"

She shrugs.

"I knew someone here killed my father if I had tits I'd never get on the inside." Bud talks more now than I've ever heard before. She's a looker, beautiful even.

I groan in irritation and look to Viper.

I just patched-in a fucking woman.

27

HARLEY

S tanding in my room, water drips down my body from the shower. I stare at my reflection in the mirror. I don't look like myself. I've lost weight, and you can even see my ribs. My eyes skim along my side and I frown seeing all the bruises on my thigh. It's ugly.

I run my fingers along the sensitive skin and wince in reaction. I wish I could have been the one to kill those assholes. Sighing, I grab the towel off the rack and twist it around me.

My room is empty and quiet. It unsettles me as where I just came from was nothing but constant screams. Where is Benji?

I look to the clock finding it to be three in the morning. I'm tired, but I want Benji to lay next to me, make me feel safe. After the mind fuck I had of him possibly being not real, I need him to be next to me as much as possible as I come to terms with what happened.

Opening my door, I head downstairs to the club, it's a ghost town. Nobody is here, not even any club escorts.

I peek in the chapel and find Benji sitting at the head of the table staring at the gavel. He looks good sitting there. Like he was born to be the president of the club. It's different not seeing my father sitting there, and a piece of me will miss him. But like Benji said. I'll miss the parts of him from when I was a little girl. The man I loved, died a long time ago.

"Benji?" I whisper. His blue eyes pop to mine and the butterflies I thought once died flutter around merciless.

"Come here, baby." He pats his lap.

Tiptoeing inside the room, I look around. I haven't been in here for years. There are mug shots on the wall of all the members, Benji's right in the middle. He looks like a bad boy with his hair in his eyes, and a 'I don't give a fuck' look on his face.

Reaching Benji I crawl into his lap, and his head falls onto my chest. His hands sliding up my back slowly.

"Are you okay?" I tangle my fingers into his dark locks of hair.

"Just a lot to take in," he mutters, his rough voice tickling my skin. Lifting his head, his hands rip off the towel and toss it to the side. I squeal and try and cover my chest. I look to the opened door.

"What if someone sees?"

"They won't." He's so sure. Grabbing me by the thighs he sets me on the wooden table and heads to the doors. Biting my bottom lip, I watch him as he strides with confidence to the double doors. He shuts them and locks them. Stepping to the metal shelf holding bullets, he turns the stereo on. He nods his head to the beat and looks over his shoulder at me.

I can't help but laugh at him. That's one thing Benji has always managed to do, make me laugh.

His eyes hooded and hungry, he comes back to me. Resting his callused hands on my knees he jerks them open. I gasp with wide eyes. Tucking an arm around my back he pulls me to him, and I wrap my legs around his strong waist.

Using his teeth, he grabs at my left nipple. The sharp pain heightening my arousal. I gasp, my hands falling to his cheeks. His skin is warm and I never want to let him go. I want his mouth on me all the time, to feel his body next to mine. My eyes roll, and my body grinds on his belt buckle.

He kisses my chest, our breathing becoming labored as we begin to lose control of our bodies. The rings on his left hand slide along my inner thigh and I open my legs wider for him. Grabbing me under the thighs he jerks my ass to the edge and lowers his head. He flicks my clit with his warm tongue and I can't help the moan spilling from my lips. My nub buzzes and tingles all the way down to my toes.

He licks and sucks at my wetness, feasting upon my arousal like a madman. My body ripples and coils with warmth and pressure. I bite and lick at my bottom lip, the sensation too much for me to handle.

His thick hot tongue feels fucking amazing against my pussy.

His thick finger suddenly fills me and my toes curl into his back. My body rocking onto his face for more friction.

"Mmmm, I could eat you for hours," he murmurs against my sensitive skin.

Using my elbows, I push myself up and watch him. The way his jaw ticks and his tongue laves at my wetness. Spit and wetness glistens across his lips and I'm so pent up I'm ready for him to just fuck me.

Tugging his hair, I rip his face from my cunt and make him face me.

"Fuck me!" I demand with a husky tone. "Fuck me, like you lost me and just got me back."

His eyes become ablaze. Grabbing onto my knee with one hand, he flips me on my stomach. My ribs clashing into the table so hard it stings. The sound of his belt buckle hitting the floor causes goosebumps to rise along my spine, my sex clenching as it knows what's about to come.

Spreading my thighs, the tip of his cock rubs back and forth amongst my heat. I groan, wrapping my feet around his ass the best I can for being on my stomach.

He thrusts inside of me so hard the entire table shakes.

"Yes!" I cry. His hand pets my back as he pushes in and out of me. That spot inside my cunt coming alive with a wave of pleasure.

"Yeah, did you miss that cock?" he growls, and I nod out of breath. The way he fills me and touches me I never want to stop fucking.

His heavy body leans over mine, his hand skirting up my side until clasps around my neck. His grip so tight I have no choice but to look right in front of me.

There's a mirror with the club colors etched into it. My cheeks are flushed and Benji looks like a fucking god hovering over me, fucking me on the very table I've wanted to be at since I was a little girl.

"See that?" he whispers behind me.

"Yeah," I moan, my body rising to the peak.

"That's my fucking queen, my bitch, the only chick that I will fuck on this table."

With his words, I come. I squeeze my eyes shut and give myself to Benji.

He slaps my butt cheek, his finger tickling the bud of my ass. This makes me tense so hard, just as I fall off the cliff of release. The wave of pleasure slamming into me, my nails dig into the wood.

Benji growls, his finger slowly sinking into my ass. Wetness drips from my pussy and I look between my legs horrified.

"What the?"

"You squirted," he informs out of breath. His cock hitting me just right over and over. The finger in my ass, causing me to clench on to his cock again as another wave of ecstasy knocks through me. My knees give out, and I collapse onto the cold table, my breathing labored and burning my lungs as I fall from the hardest orgasm I've ever had. Wetness all over my stomach, thighs, and pussy, I feel dirty and so fucking good at the same time.

Benji slowly slides out of me and I wince. It's so sensitive it hurts.

Slowly, I turn on my back and look up at my man. He smiles, his dick glistening with my wetness. My cheeks blush at what just happened. I've never done that before.

He smirks, shoving himself back in his jeans.

"That was fucking hot." He looks up through hooded eyes.

I shake my head, covering my face with my hands.

"Oh my God, no it wasn't. I can't believe I did that." I giggle, embarrassed.

Something heavy and cool falls on my bare tits and I drop my hands, my shyness fading. It's leather. There's leather in my hands.

Furrowed brows, I sit up and look the jacket over. It's brand new.

My mouth drops, it's not just a jacket. It's an ol' lady cut.

Benji's Ol' Lady, proudly stitched into it. I even have a road name.

"Hyde." Like Jekyll and Hyde. "Viper calls me Hyde." I laugh. It's perfect, it's not girly, and it's a part of me.

"I was just going to put Harley, but Viper insisted we put Hyde." Benji rubs his fingers over the new patches.

I can't stop laughing, my eyes filling with tears. I have my very own club cut. I'm a part of the club.

Benji pulls me into him, his arms feeling like home.

Looking up at him, he looks down to me.

"You think we'll be bad at this whole love thing?"

"Oh absolutely," he chuckles. His laughter fades and the giant rings on his fingers slide against my chin. I kiss them, loving him. "But I'll never stop falling in love with you."

"Even if I'm crazy?" I can't help but ask, as I try on the cut. My nipples perk amongst the cool leather.

"Never stopped me before." He shrugs, grasping the sides of my cut.

"How are you feeling?"

"I haven't had a blackout in days," I inform him. His eyes widen with surprise.

"I think accepting my love for you and remembering why Farrah was created in the process helped a lot. I feel like she is in my head, but I can hear her and listen to her rather than before where I would black out. Does that make sense?"

"It does," he mutters.

With furrowed brows, he leans in and kisses my forehead. I know what he's thinking. Just because Farrah is gone now... doesn't mean she won't be back.

She always comes back.

I'll always be crazy.

THE END

EPILOGUE

Benji

SITTING at the head of the table, Harley stands behind me, her arms resting on each side of my shoulders.

"So, did the governor pay up?" Viper asks the table.

I nod, as a cloud of smoke rolls from my lips. Bud gave me some of her hybrid stash and it's the best shit I've ever smoked. "He sent it within the hour after Harley sent the picture of them."

"Good," Viper clips.

"That smells strong." Viper looks at me with squinted eyes.

"If Bud is anything like her dad, she'll bring us in a lot of cash," my dad informs at the end of the table.

"How the hell did we not know she was a girl?" Viper asks the whole table.

I shrug. Bud hardly talked, stayed in the background. She went under the radar for sure. She's fucking smart.

"Is she patched-in?" Bridge asks, rubbing his long beard.

"She's going to show us her crops, then we can decide as a

club what to do with her," I offer, and everyone nods silently. We all feel it in our hearts that her dad was murdered, and we want to make it right. Letting her be our grower... is making it right. Hopefully.

"Does anyone else owe us money?" I ask, changing the subject.

Viper flips through the old payout books. "I'm trying to catch up and see, but it's going to take some time. Grudge hasn't updated this shit for years."

"Go fucking figure." I shake my head. Who knows what he's been stuffing in his pockets.

"A couple of the chapters in surrounding states aren't happy with how we dealt with things," Dad chimes in at the end of the table. My eyes sweep to his in knowing.

"Well, they know where to find us," I drawl out, not interested in what others think of how we run things around here.

"Where is Jessilynn?" Harley whispers in my ear from behind.

"Where is that crazy blonde chick?" I ask Viper, remembering we took a patient when we took Harley. I haven't seen her around here lately. Harley nudges me in the back, calling her friend crazy.

Viper sighs, slamming the books shut.

"We took a crazy bitch, that's for sure." He groans.

Everyone laughs at the table. I bet Viper is regretting taking her with us now.

"She's broken, she wants revenge on that hospital—"

"Did she say that?" Harley cuts in. "Did she say why she was in there?" she rambles behind me. I look to the table to see if anyone objects to her questioning, but nobody seems to mind she's in here. Probably because it feels right that she's in here. She's been here since she was a kid.

Viper shakes his head. "No, but you can see it in her eyes. She wants to hurt someone. Maybe she'll open up to you. Have you talked to her?" Viper looks at Harley.

"No, I was giving her some space. Being out of there... it's a process." She's speaking from experience. She still wakes up in the middle of the night screaming in horror. She makes me hold her all night if I so much as try and roll on my side she whimpers and makes me hold her again.

"Where is she?" I ask.

"I put her in one of the rooms down the hall."

Her brows furrow, her face falling.

"She might be twisted, but she didn't belong in that hospital," Harley informs the table.

I look over my shoulder at her, my eyes resting on hers.

"As your new president, my first order is to figure out what happened to this girl." The brothers look at me in confusion. "That asylum we found Harley in is funded by the governor. There's some shady shit happening there." I rub my chin, looking at the wooden table. "I want to do some good around this town, get the people to back us, and finding out what the fuck that place is all about, is a step in the right direction."

Harley steps up to me and grabs the gavel.

"Can I?" She looks at me with hopeful eyes. A little girl hidden in the depths. One who has wanted to slam that gavel since she was a little girl.

"Do it, baby."

Lifting her arm, she strikes the gavel into the table with the devil in her eyes and the crazy in her smile.

Fuck, I love her.

THE END

28

BONUS

BENJI'S BLUE NOTE-BOOK

Mia – Nine Years Old-

Mia likes art but doesn't like me. Her mother is a painter and her father died on the job as a fire-fighter. She always has ink or paint on her clothes, and dresses like a hippie.

Farrah – Nine Years Old-

Farrah wears dresses and heels from the club girls. She flirts with me, and every boy she comes across. Her feelings are hurt easily though, so I have to be careful. When she's upset she's the most dangerous.

Billy – Ten Years Old-

Billy is rough and likes to wrestle. He thinks the club is cool but instead of jackets, we should wear capes.

Eddie – Ten Years Old-

Eddie is a female, always covered in grease. She thinks she's twenty, and is a gearhead. Always wanting to talk about parts and the latest model of motorcycle. The things she knows is scary, I'm a boy and she knows more about bikes than I do. She's cute too.

Farrah – Ten Years Old-

Farrah came back. She was wearing a dress that was way too big and was camo. She flirted with one of the prospects boys, and I got mad. I tripped him, I'm pretty sure Farrah saw it.

Bell – Ten Years Old-

Belle wore a yellow dress. I think she thought she was literally from Beauty and The Beast. She made me braid her hair. I told her I didn't know how, but she told me to try and I tangled her hair into a rat nest. One of the club girls spent an hour combing out my mess.

Mia – Eleven Years Old-

Mia was upset about her parents being gone and wanted to try pot. So we stayed on the roof and smoke weed all day until we passed out.

Francy – Eleven Years Old-

Francy is too smart. I kept asking where she got her information but she said she just knew these things. I kept calling her Harley, and she would adjust these glasses I never knew she had and wouldn't talk to me. I started watching Harry Potter on my tablet and she sat close to me to watch over my shoulder.

I don't care what she calls herself. It was like a date with Harley.

Eddie –Twelve Years Old-

Eddie helped my dad change the spark plugs on his bike today. It was crazy watching her make her way around the garage.

Farrah – Fifteen

Farrah tried to sleep with one of the hang rounds today, and I ended up hitting him in the head with a wrench from the garage. Dad was pissed. Farrah comes and goes, but one thing is persistent. She wants love, just not with me.

Aria – Fifteen-

Very religious, scared of the club and always hides in the club's freezer. She hates the color black and makes me pray with her often. She's odd.

Farrah – Sixteen Years Old-

Farrah came forward today after Harley snapped on a girl at the gas station. She was scared and vulnerable. When they tried to take her away she clung to me. It felt good, but it's also the most scared I've ever been.

Blossom – Sixteen Years Old-

I don't know who this chick is, but she's a bitch. Says she has natural red hair and goes to charter school. Naturally, I tried to grab her ass and make her feel welcomed around the club. She was so pissed, I couldn't help but find it amusing.

Peyton – Seventeen Years Old

Angry with the world, tired of not being around kids her age and is self-destructive. She cut herself on purpose in her bathroom upstairs. I cleaned it up and even stitched her arm the best I could from a YouTube video we found so Harley's dad would never know.

Farrah – Eighteen Years Old-

Farrah came on to me today. Normally I can restrain myself, but ever since Harley gave herself to me, it's all I've thought about. I couldn't contain myself, I fucked her in my bed. The smell of her, and feel of her against me was just like my first time with Harley. Farrah acted high-class after we came, like it was just a one-time thing, but we both know she'll be back for more. Farrah is one alter that never strays.

Farrah – Nineteen Years Old-

If I noted how many times Farrah came out, this notebook would be full. She's the only alter who hasn't disappeared for good. I locked her in the room today because there was a club party. She was super slutty and fucking hot in that red dress. I had to protect what was mine.

Aria – Twenty

Oddly Aria came to the front today. I almost forgot about her, to be honest. She was scared to leave her room and made me fucking pray again. Whoever Aria is, it seems tied to the club... or maybe Grudge.

Maybe Harley knows how her dad really feels about her, and Aria is the front to deal with this?

Farrah – Twenty-Two Years Old-

Farrah walked out of her room in a towel, and I took her back to her room and fucked her into the mattress. She then said some fucked up shit about me never having Harley, and I hit the road for a much-needed ride.

Farrah – Twenty-Three Years Old-

Farrah was sitting at the bar, talking to everyone like everything was normal. She took off Harley's skull ring, and it pissed me off. I may have gotten a little rough dragging her into the club bathroom, and informing her that I'd blister her ass if she ever took it off again. It's the first time I've ever seen the look of horror cross her face.

ACKNOWLEDGMENTS

I want to thank you, the reader first. This book was so different for me, and so much fun to write. For you to take the chance on something so unique, it takes my breath away. Thank you for believing in me.

I want to thank my editor Ellie McLove next, she worked on this book in the middle of her being sick, and working on her amazing signing. She is truly fucking amazing.

My beta readers, you guys not only helped me smooth this baby out but you helped my self-confidence. I was worried sick about this book and how the readers would like it, and you all told me how amazing it would be. Thank you!

Thank you Rock Stars Of Romance, you've done amazing helping all readers and bloggers get their hands on my work.

I also need to thank my husband as one of his phrases was used in this book. One I tell myself to this day.

Thank you to my kids, as they helped too. That's right, my kids helped me write this book. They both gave me an alter for Benji's book.

NOTE FROM THE AUTHOR

Funny, this whole story started as a teacher/student romance. Something was missing though, and I couldn't put my finger on it. Then I threw in a biker to save the day, and the entire story took form.

I needed a safe haven for Harley. I needed someone to understand her, and wanted to protect her. In my heart, a club house was her home.

I did a lot of research on Dissociative Identity Disorder. In fact, it took me longer to get all the information I needed on the condition then to write the book. With that being said, my heart goes out to anyone who has been diagnosed with this. It is something that does not look easy to live with, and you are truly a soldier for your hardships.

When I was outlining this book, I made the disorder a secret at first, but then thought to myself... every book I've read on this has hidden it. Surprising the reader at the very end of what was really going on with the characters. I wanted something different, I wanted the reader to see what it's like to live in a life of confusion and black outs. So, I scrapped the whole thing and went feet first into the condition.

My book does bring to light a lot of what people with this condition go through, but Free Ride is fiction and does not in any way demonstrate to the full extent of what someone with Dissociative Identity Disorder goes through.

If the characters cooperate with me, this series will not just be about bikers. It will be about mental conditions, and sexy bikers. Shadow Keepers is a sanctuary for those who are lost after all.

Then again, my characters can be assholes and this can go a different way. So we will see...

OTHER BOOKS BY M.N. FORGY

Devils Dust MC series

What Doesn't Destroy Us Links (Devil's Dust Book 1)

The Scars That Define Us (Devil's Dust Book 2)

The Fear That Divides Us (Devil's Dust Book 3)

The Lies Between Us (Devil's Dust Book 4)

What Might Kill Us (Devil's Dust Book 5)

Sin City Outlaws MC Series

Reign (Sin City Outlaws MC 1)

Mercy (Sin City Outlaws MC 2)

Retaliate (Sin City Outlaws MC 3)

Stand alones

Relinquish

Love Tap

Plus One

STALK THE AUTHOR

Stalk her on Facebook
http://bit.ly/2u6GKHf

Stalk her on Instagram
https://www.instagram.com/m.n._forgy_author/

Sign up for her newsletter
http://mnforgy.com/newsletter/

www.mnforgy.com

Printed in Poland
by Amazon Fulfillment
Poland Sp. z o.o., Wrocław